GUILTY...

Theo hated to believe this because not a single witness had testified. Plus, he liked to tell himself that he believed in the presumption of innocence.

Guilty, Theo said again, to himself. Why couldn't he follow the law, give Mr. Duffy the benefit of innocence? Why couldn't he do what good lawyers were supposed to do? This frustrated him as he followed along behind Mr. Duffy and his lawyers.

There was something missing in the case, and based on what had already been said in court, Theo suspected that the mystery might never be solved.

READ ALL OF
THEODORE BOONE'S ADVENTURES!

JOHN GRISHAM

THEODORE BOONE
KID LAWYER

PUFFIN BOOKS

PUFFIN BOOKS
An imprint of Penguin Random House LLC, New York

First published in the United States of America by Dutton Children's Books,
an imprint of Penguin Young Readers Group, 2010
Published by Puffin Books, an imprint of Penguin Young Readers Group, 2011

Visit us online at penguinrandomhouse.com

LIBRARY OF CONGRESS CATALOGING-IN-PUBLICATION DATA IS AVAILABLE

Puffin Books 9781984816535

Designed by Irene Vandervoort

Printed in the United States of America

1 3 5 7 9 10 8 6 4 2

for Shea

CHAPTER
1

Theodore Boone was an only child and for that reason usually had breakfast alone. His father, a busy lawyer, was in the habit of leaving early and meeting friends for coffee and gossip at the same downtown diner every morning at seven. Theo's mother, herself a busy lawyer, had been trying to lose ten pounds for at least the past ten years, and because of this she'd convinced herself that breakfast should be nothing more than coffee with the newspaper. So he ate by himself at the kitchen table, cold cereal and orange juice, with an eye on the clock. The Boone home had clocks everywhere, clear evidence of organized people.

Actually, he wasn't completely alone. Beside his chair, his dog ate, too. Judge was a thoroughly mixed mutt whose age and breeding would always be a mystery. Theo had rescued him from near death with a last-second appearance in Animal Court two years earlier, and Judge would always be grateful. He preferred Cheerios, same as Theo, and they ate together in silence every morning.

At 8:00 a.m., Theo rinsed their bowls in the sink, placed the milk and juice back in the fridge, walked to the den, and kissed his mother on the cheek. "Off to school," he said.

"Do you have lunch money?" she asked, the same question five mornings a week.

"Always."

"And your homework is complete?"

"It's perfect, Mom."

"And I'll see you when?"

"I'll stop by the office after school." Theo stopped by the office every day after school, without fail, but Mrs. Boone always asked.

"Be careful," she said. "And remember to smile." The braces on his teeth had now been in place for over two years and Theo wanted desperately to get rid of them. In the meantime, though, his mother continually reminded him to smile and make the world a happier place.

"I'm smiling, Mom."

"Love you, Teddy."

"Love you back."

Theo, still smiling in spite of being called "Teddy," flung his backpack across his shoulders, scratched Judge on the head and said good-bye, then left through the kitchen door. He hopped on his bike and was soon speeding down Mallard Lane, a narrow leafy street in the oldest section of town. He waved at Mr. Nunnery, who was already on his porch and settled in for another long day of watching what little traffic found its way into their neighborhood, and he whisked by Mrs. Goodloe at the curb without speaking because she'd lost her hearing and most of her mind as well. He did smile at her, though, but she did not return the smile. Her teeth were somewhere in the house.

It was early spring and the air was crisp and cool. Theo pedaled quickly, the wind stinging his face. Homeroom was at eight forty and he had important matters before school. He cut through a side street, darted down an alley, dodged some traffic, and ran a stop sign. This was Theo's turf, the route he traveled every day. After four blocks the houses gave way to offices and shops and stores.

The county courthouse was the largest building in downtown Strattenburg (the post office was second, the library third). It sat majestically on the north side of Main Street, halfway between a bridge over the river and a park filled with gazebos and birdbaths and monuments to those killed in wars. Theo loved the courthouse, with its air of authority, and people hustling importantly about, and somber notices and schedules tacked to the bulletin boards. Most of all, Theo loved the courtrooms themselves. There were small ones where more private matters were handled without juries, then there was the main courtroom on the second floor where lawyers battled like gladiators and judges ruled like kings.

At the age of thirteen, Theo was still undecided about his future. One day he dreamed of being a famous trial lawyer, one who handled the biggest cases and never lost before juries. The next day he dreamed of being a great judge, noted for his wisdom and fairness. He went back and forth, changing his mind daily.

The main lobby was already busy on this Monday morning, as if the lawyers and their clients wanted an early start to the week. There was a crowd waiting by the elevator, so Theo raced up two flights of stairs and down the east wing where Family Court was held. His mother was a noted divorce lawyer, one who always represented the wife, and Theo knew this area of the building well. Since divorce trials were decided by judges, juries were not used, and since most judges preferred not to have large groups of spectators observing such sensitive matters, the courtroom was small. By its door, several lawyers huddled importantly, obviously not agreeing on much. Theo searched the hallway, then turned a corner and saw his friend.

She was sitting on one of the old wooden benches, alone, small and frail and nervous. When she saw him she smiled and put a hand over her mouth. Theo hustled over and sat next to her, very closely, knees touching. With any other girl he would have placed himself at least two feet away and prevented any chance of contact.

But April Finnemore was not just any girl. They had started prekindergarten together at the age of four at a nearby church school, and they had been close friends since they could remember. It wasn't a romance; they were too young for that. Theo did not know of a single thirteen-year-old boy in his class who admitted to having a girlfriend. Just the opposite. They wanted nothing to do with them. And the girls felt the same way. Theo had been warned that things would change, and dramatically, but that seemed unlikely.

April was just a friend, and one in a great deal of need at the moment. Her parents were divorcing, and Theo was extremely grateful his mother was not involved with the case.

The divorce was no surprise to anyone who knew the Finnemores. April's father was an eccentric antiques dealer and the drummer for an old rock band that still played in nightclubs and toured for weeks at a time. Her mother raised goats and made goat cheese, which she peddled around town in a converted funeral hearse, painted bright yellow. An ancient spider monkey with gray whiskers rode shotgun and munched on the cheese, which had never sold very well. Mr. Boone had once described the family as "nontraditional," which Theo took to mean downright weird. Both her parents had been arrested on drug charges, though neither had served time.

"Are you okay?" Theo asked.

"No," she said. "I hate being here."

She had an older brother named August and an older sister named March, and both fled the family. August left the day after he graduated from high school. March dropped out at the age of sixteen and left town, leaving April as the only child for her parents to torment. Theo knew all of this because April told him everything. She had to. She needed someone outside of her family to confide in, and Theo was her listener.

"I don't want to live with either one of them," she said. It was a terrible thing to say about one's parents, but Theo understood completely. He despised her parents for the way they treated her. He despised them for the chaos of their lives, for their neglect of April, for their cruelty to her. Theo had a long list of grudges against Mr. and Mrs. Finnemore. He would run away before being forced to live there. He did not know of a single kid in town who'd ever set foot inside the Finnemore home.

The divorce trial was in its third day, and April would soon be called to the witness stand to testify. The judge would ask her the fateful question, "April, which parent do you want to live with?"

And she did not know the answer. She had discussed it for hours with Theo, and she still did not know what to say.

The great question in Theo's mind was, "Why did either parent want custody of April?" Each had neglected her in so many ways. He had heard many stories, but he had never repeated a single one.

"What are you going to say?" he asked.

"I'm telling the judge that I want to live with my aunt Peg in Denver."

"I thought she said no."

"She did."

"Then you can't say that."

"What can I say, Theo?"

"My mother would say that you should choose your mother. I know she's not your first choice, but you don't have a first choice."

"But the judge can do whatever he wants, right?"

"Right. If you were fourteen, you could make a binding decision. At thirteen, the judge will only consider your wishes. According to my mother, this judge almost never awards custody to the father. Play it safe. Go with your mother."

April wore jeans, hiking boots, and a navy sweater. She rarely dressed like a girl, but her gender was never in doubt. She wiped a tear from her cheek, but managed to keep her composure. "Thanks, Theo," she said.

"I wish I could stay."

"And I wish I could go to school."

They both managed a forced laugh. "I'll be thinking about you. Be strong."

"Thanks, Theo."

His favorite judge was the Honorable Henry Gantry, and he entered the great man's outer office at twenty minutes after 8:00 a.m.

"Well, good morning, Theo," Mrs. Hardy said. She was stirring something into her coffee and preparing to begin her work.

"Morning, Mrs. Hardy," Theo said with a smile.

"And to what do we owe this honor?" she asked. She

was not quite as old as Theo's mother, he guessed, and she was very pretty. She was Theo's favorite of all the secretaries in the courthouse. His favorite clerk was Jenny over in Family Court.

"I need to see Judge Gantry," he replied. "Is he in?"

"Well, yes, but he's very busy."

"Please. It'll just take a minute."

She sipped her coffee, then asked, "Does this have anything to do with the big trial tomorrow?"

"Yes, ma'am, it does. I'd like for my Government class to watch the first day of the trial, but I gotta make sure there will be enough seats."

"Oh, I don't know about that, Theo," Mrs. Hardy said, frowning and shaking her head. "We're expecting an overflow crowd. Seating will be tight."

"Can I talk to the judge?"

"How many are in your class?"

"Sixteen. I thought maybe we could sit in the balcony."

She was still frowning as she picked up the phone and pushed a button. She waited for a second, then said, "Yes, Judge, Theodore Boone is here and would like to see you. I told him you are very busy." She listened some more, then put down the phone. "Hurry," she said, pointing to the judge's door.

Seconds later, Theo stood before the biggest desk in town,

a desk covered with all sorts of papers and files and thick binders, a desk that symbolized the enormous power held by Judge Henry Gantry, who, at that moment, was not smiling. In fact, Theo was certain the judge had not cracked a smile since he'd interrupted his work. Theo, though, was pressing hard with a prolonged flash of metal from ear to ear.

"State your case," Judge Gantry said. Theo had heard him issue this command on many occasions. He'd seen lawyers, good lawyers, rise and stutter and search for words while Judge Gantry scowled down from the bench. He wasn't scowling now, nor was he wearing his black robe, but he was still intimidating. As Theo cleared his throat, he saw an unmistakable twinkle in his friend's eye.

"Yes, sir, well, my Government teacher is Mr. Mount, and Mr. Mount thinks we might get approval from the principal for an all-day field trip to watch the opening of the trial tomorrow." Theo paused, took a deep breath, told himself again to speak clearly, slowly, forcefully, like all great trial lawyers. "But, we need guaranteed seats. I was thinking we could sit in the balcony."

"Oh, you were?"

"Yes, sir."

"How many?"

"Sixteen, plus Mr. Mount."

The judge picked up a file, opened it, and began reading

as if he'd suddenly forgotten about Theo standing at attention across the desk. Theo waited for an awkward fifteen seconds. Then the judge abruptly said, "Seventeen seats, front balcony, left side. I'll tell the bailiff to seat you at ten minutes before nine, tomorrow. I expect perfect behavior."

"No problem, sir."

"I'll have Mrs. Hardy e-mail a note to your principal."

"Thanks, Judge."

"You can go now, Theo. Sorry to be so busy."

"No problem, sir."

Theo was scurrying toward the door when the judge said, "Say, Theo. Do you think Mr. Duffy is guilty?"

Theo stopped, turned around and without hesitating responded, "He's presumed innocent."

"Got that. But what's your opinion as to his guilt?"

"I think he did it."

The judge nodded slightly but gave no indication of whether he agreed.

"What about you?" Theo asked.

Finally, a smile. "I'm a fair and impartial referee, Theo. I have no preconceived notions of guilt or innocence."

"That's what I thought you'd say."

"See you tomorrow." Theo cracked the door and hustled out.

Mrs. Hardy was on her feet, hands on hips, staring

down two flustered lawyers who were demanding to see the judge. All three clammed up when Theo walked out of Judge Gantry's office. He smiled at Mrs. Hardy as he walked hurriedly by. "Thanks," he said as he opened the door and disappeared.

CHAPTER 2

The ride from the courthouse to the middle school would take fifteen minutes if properly done, if one obeyed the traffic laws and refrained from trespassing. And normally this is the way Theo would do things, except when he was running a bit late. He flew down Market Street the wrong way, jumped the curb just ahead of a car, and bolted through a parking lot, used every sidewalk available, then—his most serious offense—he ducked between two houses on Elm Street. Theo heard someone yelling from the porch behind him until he was safely into an alley that ran into the teachers' parking lot behind his school. He checked his watch—nine minutes. Not bad.

He parked at the rack by the flagpole, secured his bike
with a chain, then entered with a flood of kids who'd just
stepped off a bus. The eight forty bell was ringing when he
walked into his homeroom and said good morning to Mr.
Mount, who not only taught him Government but was his
adviser as well.

"Talked to Judge Gantry," Theo said at the teacher's
desk, one considerably smaller than the one he'd just left
in the courthouse. The room was buzzing with the usual
early morning chaos. All sixteen boys were present and all
appeared to be involved in some sort of gag, scuffle, joke, or
shoving match.

"And?"

"Got the seats, first thing in the morning."

"Excellent. Great job, Theo."

Mr. Mount eventually restored order, called the roll,
made his announcements, and ten minutes later sent the
boys down the hall to their first period Spanish class with
Madame Monique. There was some awkward flirting
between the rooms as the boys mixed with the girls. During
classes, they were "gender-separated," according to a new
policy adopted by the smart people in charge of educating
all the children in town. The genders were free to mingle at
all other times.

Madame Monique was a tall, dark lady from Cameroon, in West Africa. She had moved to Strattenburg three years earlier when her husband, also from Cameroon, took a job at the local college where he taught languages. She was not the typical teacher at the middle school, far from it. As a child in Africa, she had grown up speaking Beti, her tribal dialect, as well as French and English, the official languages of Cameroon. Her father was a doctor, and thus could afford to send her to school in Switzerland, where she picked up German and Italian. Her Spanish had been perfected when she went to college in Madrid. She was currently working on Russian with plans to move on to Mandarin Chinese. Her classroom was filled with large, colorful maps of the world, and her students believed she'd been everywhere, seen everything, and could speak any language. It's a big world, she told them many times, and most people in other countries speak more than one language. While the students concentrated on Spanish, they were also encouraged to explore others.

Theo's mother had been studying Spanish for twenty years, and as a preschooler he had learned from her many of the basic words and phrases. Some of her clients were from Central America, and when Theo saw them at the office he was ready to practice. They always thought it was cute.

Madame Monique had told him that he had an ear for

languages, and this had inspired him to study harder. She was often asked by her curious students to "say something in German." Or, "Speak some Italian." She would, but first the student making the request had to stand and say a few words in that language. Bonus points were given, and this created enthusiasm. Most of the boys in Theo's class knew a few dozen words in several languages. Aaron, who had a Spanish mother and a German father, was by far the most talented linguist. But Theo was determined to catch him. After Government, Spanish was his favorite class, and Madame Monique ran a close second to Mr. Mount as his favorite teacher.

Today, though, he had trouble concentrating. They were studying Spanish verbs, a tedious chore on a good day, and Theo's mind was elsewhere. He worried about April and her awful day on the witness stand. He couldn't imagine the horror of being forced to choose one parent over another. And when he managed to set April aside, he was consumed with the murder trial and couldn't wait until tomorrow, to watch the opening statements by the lawyers.

Most of his classmates dreamed of getting tickets to the big game or concert. Theo Boone lived for the big trials.

Second period was Geometry with Miss Garman. It was followed by a short break outdoors, then the class returned to homeroom, to Mr. Mount and the best hour of the day, at least in Theo's opinion. Mr. Mount was in his midthirties, and had once worked as a lawyer at a gigantic firm in a skyscraper in Chicago. His brother was a lawyer. His father and grandfather had been lawyers and judges. Mr. Mount, though, had grown weary of the long hours and high pressure, and, well, he'd quit. He'd walked away from the big money and found something he found far more rewarding. He loved teaching, and though he still thought of himself as a lawyer, he considered the classroom far more important than the courtroom.

Because he knew the law so well, his Government class spent most of its time discussing cases, old ones and current ones and even fictitious ones on television.

"All right, men," he began when they were seated and still. He always addressed them as "men" and for thirteen-year-olds there was no greater compliment. "Tomorrow I want you here at eight fifteen. We'll take a bus to the courthouse and we'll be in our seats in plenty of time. It's a field trip, approved by the principal, so you will be excused from all other classes. Bring lunch money and we'll eat at Pappy's Deli. Any questions?"

The men were hanging on every word, excitement all over their faces.

"What about backpacks?" someone asked.

"No," Mr. Mount answered. "You can't take anything into the courtroom. Security will be tight. It is, after all, the first murder trial here in a long time. Any more questions?"

"What should we wear?"

Slowly, all eyes turned to Theo, including those of Mr. Mount. It was well known that Theo spent more time in the courthouse than most lawyers.

"Coat and tie, Theo?" Mr. Mount asked.

"No, not at all. What we're wearing now is fine."

"Great. Any more questions? Good. Now, I've asked Theo if he would sort of set the stage for tomorrow. Lay out the courtroom, give us the players, tell us what we're in for. Theo."

Theo's laptop was already wired to the overhead projector. He walked to the front of the class, pressed a key, and a large diagram appeared on the digital wide-screen whiteboard. "This is the main courtroom," Theo said, in his best lawyer's voice. He held a laser pointer with a red light and sort of waved it around the diagram. "At the top, in the center here, is the bench. That's where the judge sits and controls the trial. Not sure why it's called a bench. It's more like a throne. But, anyway, we'll stick with bench. The judge is Henry Gantry." He punched a key, and a large formal photo of Judge Gantry appeared. Black robe, somber face. Theo shrank it, then dragged it up to the bench. With the judge in place, he continued, "Judge Gantry has been a judge for about twenty years and handles only criminal cases. He runs a tight courtroom and is well liked by most of the lawyers." The laser pointer moved to the middle of the courtroom. "This is the defense table, where Mr. Duffy, the man accused of murder, will be seated." Theo punched a key and a black-and-white photo, one taken from a newspaper, appeared. "This is Mr. Duffy. Age forty-nine, used to be married to Mrs. Duffy, who is now deceased, and as we all know, Mr. Duffy is accused of murdering her." He shrank the photo and moved it to the defense table. "His lawyer is Clifford Nance, probably the top criminal defense lawyer in this part of the state." Nance appeared in color, wearing a dark suit and a shifty smile. He had long, curly gray hair. His photo was reduced and placed next to his client's. "Next to the defense table is the prosecution's table. The lead prosecutor is Jack Hogan, who's also known as the district attorney, or DA." Hogan's photo appeared for a few seconds before it was reduced and placed at the table next to the defense.

"Where'd you find these photos?" someone asked.

"Each year the bar association publishes a directory of all the lawyers and judges," Theo answered.

"Are you included?" This brought a few light laughs.

"No. Now, there will be other lawyers and paralegals at both tables, prosecution and defense. This area is usually crowded. Over here, next to the defense, is the jury box. It has fourteen chairs—twelve for the jurors and two for the alternates. Most states still use twelve-man juries, though different sizes are not unusual. Regardless of the number, the verdict has to be unanimous, at least in criminal cases. They pick alternates in case one of the twelve gets sick or excused or something. The jury was selected last week, so we won't have to watch that. It's pretty boring." The laser pointer moved to a spot in front of the bench. Theo continued, "The court reporter sits here. She'll have a machine that is called a stenograph. Sorta looks like a typewriter, but much different. Her job is to record every word that's said during the trial. That might sound impossible, but she makes it look easy. Later, she'll prepare what's known as a transcript so that the lawyers and the judge will have a record of everything. Some transcripts have thousands of pages." The laser pointer moved again. "Here, close to the court reporter and just down from the judge, is the witness chair. Each witness walks up here, is sworn to tell the truth, then takes a seat."

"Where do we sit?"

The laser pointer moved to the middle of the diagram. "This is called the bar. Again, don't ask why. The bar is a wooden railing that separates the spectators from the trial area. There are ten rows of seats with an aisle down the middle. This is usually more than enough for the crowd, but this trial will be different." The laser pointer moved to the rear of the courtroom. "Up here, above the last few rows, is the balcony where there are three long benches. We're in the balcony, but don't worry. We'll be able to see and hear everything."

"Any questions?" Mr. Mount asked.

The boys gawked at the diagram. "Who goes first?" someone asked.

Theo began pacing. "Well, the State has the burden of proving guilt, so it must present its case first. First thing tomorrow morning, the prosecutor will walk to the jury box and address the jurors. This is called the opening statement. He'll lay out his case. Then the defense lawyer will do the same. After that, the State will start calling witnesses. As you know, Mr. Duffy is presumed to be innocent, so the State must prove him guilty, and it must do so beyond a reasonable doubt. He claims he's innocent, which actually in real life doesn't happen very often. About eighty percent of those indicted for murder eventually plead guilty, because they are in fact guilty. The other twenty percent go to trial, and ninety percent of those are found guilty. So, it's rare for a murder defendant to be found not guilty."

"My dad thinks he's guilty," Brian said.

"A lot of people do," Theo said.

"How many trials have you watched, Theo?"

"I don't know. Dozens."

Since none of the other fifteen had ever seen the inside of a courtroom, this was almost beyond belief. Theo continued: "For those of you who watch a lot of television, don't expect fireworks. A real trial is very different, and not nearly as exciting. There are no surprise witnesses, no dramatic confessions, no fistfights between the lawyers. And, in this trial, there are no eyewitnesses to the murder. This means that all of the evidence from the State will be circumstantial. You'll hear this word a lot, especially from Mr. Clifford Nance, the defense lawyer. He'll make a big deal out of the fact that the State has no direct proof, that everything is circumstantial."

"I'm not sure what that means," someone said.

"It means that the evidence is indirect, not direct. For example, did you ride your bike to school?"

"Yes."

"And did you chain it to the rack by the flagpole?"

"Yes."

"So, when you leave school this afternoon, and you go to the rack, and your bike is gone, and the chain has been cut, then you have indirect evidence that someone stole your bike. No one saw the thief, so there's no direct evidence. And let's say that tomorrow the police find your bike in a pawnshop on Raleigh Street, a place known to deal in stolen bikes. The owner gives the police a name, they investigate and find some dude with a history of stealing bikes. You can then make a strong case, through indirect evidence, that this guy is your thief. No direct evidence, but circumstantial."

Even Mr. Mount was nodding along. He was the faculty adviser for the Eighth-Grade Debate Team, and, not surprisingly, Theodore Boone was his star. He'd never had a student as quick on his feet.

"Thank you, Theo," Mr. Mount said. "And thank you for getting us the seats in the morning."

"Nothing to it," Theo said, and proudly took his seat.

It was a bright class in a strong public school. Justin was by far the best athlete, though he couldn't swim as fast as Brian. Ricardo beat them all at golf and tennis. Edward played the cello, Woody the electric guitar, Darren the drums, Jarvis the trumpet. Joey had the highest IQ and made perfect grades. Chase was the mad scientist who was always a threat to blow up the lab. Aaron spoke Spanish, from his mother's side, German from his father's, and English, of course. Brandon had an early morning paper route, traded stocks online, and planned to be the first millionaire in the group.

Naturally, there were two hopeless nerds and at least one potential felon.

The class even had its own lawyer, a first for Mr. Mount.

CHAPTER
3

The law firm of Boone & Boone had its offices in an old converted house on Park Street, three blocks off of Main and a ten-minute walk to the courthouse. There were lots of lawyers in the neighborhood, and all the houses on Park had become the offices of attorneys, architects, accountants, engineers, and so on.

The firm had two lawyers, Mr. Boone and Mrs. Boone, and they were equal partners in every sense of the word. Mr. Boone, Theo's father, was in his early fifties, but seemed to be much older, at least in Theo's well-kept opinion. His first name was Woods, which, to Theo, seemed more suited for a surname. Tiger Woods, the golfer. James Woods, the actor. Theo was still searching for another human being with the first name of Woods, though he didn't spend a lot of time worrying about this slight nuisance. He tried not to worry about things out of his control.

Woods Boone. Sometimes, Theo pronounced the name quickly and it sounded like woodspoon. He'd checked and woodspoon wasn't really a word, but he thought it should be. A spoon made from wood is known as a wooden spoon, not a woodspoon. But who uses a wooden spoon? Why worry about such trivial matters? Anyway, like one of those annoying habits you can't break, Theo thought of the word *woodspoon* every time he approached the door to his father's office and saw his name stenciled in black lettering.

His office was on the second floor, up some rickety steps covered with stained and threadbare carpet. Mr. Boone was on the second floor, alone, because the ladies below had sent him there for two reasons. First, he was a slob and his office was a wreck, though Theo loved it. Second, and much more offensive, Mr. Boone smoked a pipe, and preferred to do so with the windows closed and the ceiling fan off so that the air was thick with the rich aroma of whatever flavored tobacco he happened to favor that day. The smoke didn't bother Theo, either, though he did worry about his father's health. Mr. Boone was not exactly concerned with fitness. He exercised little and was a bit on the heavy side. He worked hard but left his problems at the office, unlike his law partner, Theo's mom.

Mr. Boone was a real estate lawyer, and in Theo's opinion this was the most boring of all areas of the law. His father never went to court, never argued before a judge, never addressed a jury, never, it seemed, left the office. In fact, he often referred to himself as an "office lawyer," and appeared pleased with such a title. Theo certainly admired his father, but he had no plans to spend his career locked away in some office. No, sir. Theo was headed for the courtroom.

Because Mr. Boone was alone on the second floor, his office was huge. Long, saggy bookshelves lined two of the walls and on the other two were ever-expanding collections of framed photographs depicting Woods doing all sorts of important things—shaking hands with politicians, posing with lawyers at bar meetings, and so on. Theo had seen the inside of several other lawyers' offices in town—he was quite nosy and always looking for an open door—and he'd already learned that lawyers loved to cover their walls with such photos, along with diplomas and awards and certificates of membership in this club or that. The Ego Wall, his mother called it, sneering, because her walls were practically bare, with only a few pieces of some baffling modern art hanging about.

Theo knocked on the door as he pushed it open. He was expected to say hello to both parents each afternoon after school, unless he was busy elsewhere. His father sat alone behind an ancient desk that was covered with piles of paper. His father was always alone because his clients seldom stopped by. They called or sent stuff by mail or fax or e-mail, but they didn't need to visit Boone & Boone to get advice.

"Hello," Theo said as he fell into a chair.

"A good day at school?" his father asked, the same question every day.

"Pretty good. The principal approved our field trip to go to court tomorrow. I saw Judge Gantry this morning and he promised seats in the balcony."

"That was nice. You're lucky. Half the town will be there."

"Are you going?"

"Me? No," his father said, waving at the piles of paper as if they required immediate attention. Theo had overheard a conversation between his parents in which they had vowed not to stop by the courtroom during the murder trial. They were busy lawyers themselves, and, well, it just didn't seem right to waste time watching someone else's trial. But Theo knew that they, like everyone else in town, wanted to be there.

His father, and his mother to a lesser extent, used the excuse of too much legal work when they wanted to avoid doing something.

"How long will the trial last?" Theo asked.

"The word on the street is that it might take a week."

"I'd sure like to watch all of it."

"Don't even think about it, Theo. I've already talked to Judge Gantry. If he sees you in the courtroom when you're supposed to be in school, he will stop the trial, order a bailiff to take you into custody, and haul you away. I will not bail you out of jail. You'll sit there for days with common drunks and gang members."

With that, Mr. Boone picked up a pipe, fired a small torch into its bowl, and began blowing smoke. They stared at each other. Theo wasn't sure if his father was joking, but his face certainly looked serious. He and Judge Gantry were old friends.

"Are you kidding?" Theo finally asked.

"Partially. I'm sure I'd fetch you from jail, but I have talked to Judge Gantry."

Theo was already thinking of ways to watch the trial without being seen by Judge Gantry. Skipping school would be the easy part.

"Now shove off," Mr. Boone said. "Let's get the home-work done."

"See you later."

Downstairs, the front door was guarded by a woman who was almost as old as the office itself. Her first name was Elsa. Her last name was Miller, though this was off-limits to Theo and everyone else. Regardless of her age, and no one knew it for certain, she insisted on being called Elsa. Even by a thirteen-year-old. Elsa had worked for the Boones since long before Theo was born. She was the receptionist, secretary, office manager, and paralegal when needed. She ran the firm, and occasionally she was forced to referee the little spats and disagreements between lawyer Boone upstairs and lawyer Boone downstairs.

Elsa was a very important person in the lives of all three Boones. Theo considered her a friend and confidante. "Hello, Elsa," he said as he stopped at her desk and prepared to give her a hug.

She jumped from her chair, bubbly as always, and squeezed him tightly. Then she looked at his chest and said, "Didn't you wear that shirt Friday?"

"I did not." And he did not.

"I think you did."

"Sorry, Elsa." She often commented on his attire, and, for a thirteen-year-old boy this was tiresome. However, it kept Theo on his toes. Someone was always watching and taking notes, and he often thought of Elsa when he hurriedly got dressed each morning. Another irritating habit he couldn't shake.

Her own wardrobe was legendary. She was short and very petite—"could wear anything," his mother had said many times—and preferred tight clothing in bold colors. Today, she was wearing black leather pants with some sort of funky green sweater that reminded Theo of asparagus. Her short gray hair was shiny and spiked. Her eyeglasses, as always, matched the color of her outfit—green today. Elsa was anything but dull. She might be pushing seventy, but she was not aging quietly.

"Is my mother in?" Theo asked.

"Yes, and the door is open." She was back in her chair. Theo was walking away.

"Thank you."

"One of your friends called."

"Who?"

"Said his name was Sandy and he might be stopping by."

"Thanks."

Theo walked along the hallway. He stopped at one door and said hello to Dorothy, the real estate secretary, a nice lady who was as boring as her boss upstairs. He stopped at another door and said hello to Vince, their longtime paralegal who worked on Mrs. Boone's cases.

Marcella Boone was on the phone when Theo walked

in and took a seat. Her desk, glass and chrome, was neatly organized with most of the surface visible, a sharp contrast to her husband's. Her current files were in a tidy rack behind her. Everything was in place, except her shoes, which were not on her feet but parked nearby. The shoes were heels, which to Theo meant that she had been in court during the day. She was in a courtroom outfit—a burgundy skirt and jacket. His mother was always pretty and put together, but she made an extra effort on those days when she went to court.

"The men can look like slobs," she said many times. "But the women are expected to look nice. What's fair about that?"

Elsa always agreed that it wasn't fair.

The truth was that Mrs. Boone enjoyed spending money on clothes and looking nice. Mr. Boone cared nothing for fashion and even less for neatness. He was only three years older in age, but at least a decade in spirit.

At the moment, she was talking to a judge, one who did not agree with her. When she finally hung up, her attitude changed quickly. With a smile she said, "Hello, my dear. How was your day?"

"Great, Mom. And yours?"

"The usual. Any excitement at school?"

"Just a field trip tomorrow, to watch the trial. Are you going?"

She was already shaking her head no. "I have a hearing at ten in front of Judge Sanford. I'm too busy to sit through a trial, Theo."

"Dad says he's already talked to Judge Gantry, and they've cooked up a plan to keep me away from the trial. Do you believe it?"

"I certainly hope so. School is a priority."

"School is boring, Mom. I enjoy two classes. Everything else is a waste of time."

"I wouldn't say your education is a waste."

"I can learn more in the courtroom."

"Perhaps, but you'll have a chance to spend plenty of time there one day. For now, though, we're concentrating on the eighth grade. Okay?"

"I'm thinking about taking a few law courses online. There's a cool website that offers some great stuff."

"Theodore, honey, you're not ready for law school. We've had this conversation. Let's enjoy the eighth grade, then off to high school, then beyond. You're just a kid, okay? Enjoy being a kid."

He sort of shrugged, said nothing.

"Now, let's get the homework done."

Her phone buzzed and Elsa was sending back another important call. "Now, excuse me, Teddy, and please smile," Mrs. Boone said. Theo eased out of the office. He carried his backpack through the copy room, always a mess, and worked his way through two storage rooms packed with large boxes of old files.

Theo was certain that he was the only eighth grader in Strattenburg with his own law office. It was a small boxlike closet that someone had added to the main house decades earlier, and before Theo took it over the firm had used it to store old law books that were out of date. His desk was a card table that was not quite as neat as his mother's but much more organized than his father's. His chair was a ragged swivel unit he'd saved from the junk pile when his parents had refurbished the library up front near Elsa's station.

Sitting in his chair was his dog. Judge spent each day at the office, sleeping or roaming quietly around, trying to avoid the humans because they were always so busy. He was routinely kicked out of meetings. Late in the day, he eased back to Theo's office, climbed into his chair, and waited.

"Hello, Judge," Theo said as he rubbed his head. "Have you had a busy day?"

Judge jumped to the floor, tail wagging, a very happy dog. Theo settled into his chair and put his backpack on the desk. He looked around the room. On one wall he'd tacked a large Twins poster with this season's schedule. To his knowledge, he was the only Twins fan in town. Minnesota was a thousand miles away and Theo had never been there. He pulled for the team because no one else in Strattenburg did so. He felt it only fair that they have at least one fan in town. He'd chosen the Twins years earlier, and now clung to them with a fierce loyalty that was tested throughout the long season.

On another wall, there was a large, cartoonish sketch of Theo Boone, Attorney-at-Law, wearing a suit and a tie and standing in court. A gavel was flying by his head, barely missing him, and the caption read, "Overruled!" In the background, the jurors were howling with laughter, at Theo's expense. At the bottom right-hand corner the artist had scribbled her name, *April Finnemore*. She had given the sketch to Theo a year earlier, for his birthday. Her dream was to run away to Paris now, and spend the rest of her life drawing and painting street scenes.

A door led to a small porch that led to the backyard, which was covered with gravel and used for parking.

As usual, he unloaded his backpack and started his homework, which had to be finished before dinner, according to a rather rigid rule established by his parents when he was in the first grade. An asthma condition kept Theo away from the team sports he longed to play, but it also ensured straight A's in school. Over the years, he had grudgingly accepted the fact that his academic success was a good substitute for the games he missed. He could play golf, though, and he and his father teed off every Saturday morning at nine.

There was a knock on the back door. Judge, who kept a bed under the desk, growled softly.

Sandy Coe was also in the eighth grade at the middle school, but in a different section. Theo knew him but not well. He was a pleasant boy who said little. He needed to talk, and Theo welcomed him to his room. Sandy took the only other chair, a folding one that Theo kept in a corner. When they were both seated, the room was full.

"Can we talk in private?" Sandy asked. He seemed shy, and nervous.

"Sure. What's up?"

"Well, I need some advice, I think. I'm really not sure about this, but I gotta talk to someone."

Theo, the counselor, said, "I promise anything you say is kept in secret."

"Good. Well, my dad got laid off a few months ago, and, well, things are pretty bad around the house." He paused, waiting for Theo to say something.

"I'm sorry."

"And last night my parents were having this real serious talk in the kitchen, and I should not have been listening, but I couldn't help it. Do you know what foreclosure means?"

"Yes."

"What is it?"

"There are a lot of foreclosures these days. It means that a person who owns a home can't make the mortgage payments and the bank wants to take the house."

"I don't understand any of this."

"Okay. It works like this." Theo grabbed a paperback and placed it in the center of his desk. "Let's say that this is a house and you want to buy it. It costs a hundred thousand dollars, and since you don't have a hundred thousand dollars, you go to the bank and borrow the money." He placed a textbook next to the paperback. "This is the bank."

"Got it."

"The bank loans you the hundred thousand, and now you're able to buy the house from whoever is selling it. You agree to pay the bank, say five hundred dollars a month, for thirty years."

"Thirty years?"

"Yep. That's the typical deal. The bank charges an extra fee for making the loan—it's called interest—so each month you pay back part of the hundred thousand plus a chunk for interest. It's a good deal for everybody. You get the house you want, and the bank makes money on the interest. All is well until something happens and you can't make the monthly payments."

"What's a mortgage?"

"A deal like this is called a mortgage. The bank has a claim on the house until the loan is paid off. When you fall behind on the monthly payments, the bank has the right to come in and take the house. The bank kicks you out, and it owns the house. That's a foreclosure." He placed the textbook on top of the paperback, smothering it.

"My mom was crying when they were talking about moving out. We've lived there since I was born."

Theo opened his laptop and turned it on. "It's terrible," he said. "And it's happening a lot these days."

Sandy lowered his head and appeared to be devastated.

"What's your father's name?"

"Thomas. Thomas Coe."

"And your mother?"

"Evelyn."

Theo pecked away. "What's your address?"

"Eight fourteen Bennington."

More pecking. They waited, then Theo said, "Oh boy."

"What is it?"

"The bank is Security Trust, on Main Street. Fourteen years ago your parents borrowed a hundred and twenty thousand for a thirty-year mortgage. They have not made the monthly payments in four months."

"Four months?"

"Yep."

"All this stuff is online?"

"Yes, but not just anybody can find it."

"How'd you find it?"

"There are ways. A lot of law offices pay a fee to gain access to certain data. Plus, I know how to dig a little deeper."

Sandy sank even lower and shook his head. "So we're gonna lose our house?"

"Not exactly."

"What do you mean? My dad's not working."

"There's a way to stop the foreclosure, stiff-arm the bank, and keep the house for a while, maybe until your dad goes back to work."

Sandy looked thoroughly bewildered.

"You ever heard of bankruptcy?" Theo asked.

"I guess, but I don't understand it."

"It's your only choice. Your parents will be forced to file for bankruptcy protection. This means they hire a lawyer who'll file some papers in Bankruptcy Court on their behalf."

"How much do lawyers cost?"

"Don't worry about that now. The important thing is to go see a lawyer."

"You can't do it?"

"Sorry. And my parents are not bankruptcy lawyers. But there is a guy two doors down, Steve Mozingo, and he's very good. My parents send clients to him. They like him a lot."

Sandy scribbled down the name. "And you think we might get to keep our house?"

"Yes, but your parents need to see this guy as soon as possible."

"Thanks, Theo. I don't know what to say."

"No problem. Happy to help."

Sandy hurried through the door, as if he might sprint home with the good news. Theo watched him get on his bike and disappear through the back parking lot.

Another satisfied client.

CHAPTER 4

At fifteen minutes before 5:00 p.m., Mrs. Boone walked into Theo's office with a folder in one hand and a document in another. "Theo," she said, her reading glasses halfway down her nose. "Would you run these over to Family Court and get them filed before five?"

"Sure, Mom."

Theo was on his feet, reaching for his backpack. He had been hoping that from some corner of the firm someone would need something filed in the courthouse.

"Your homework is finished, isn't it?"

"Yes. I didn't have much."

"Good. And today is Monday. You'll pay a visit to Ike, won't you? It means a lot to him."

Every Monday of his life, Theo was reminded by his mother that the day was in fact Monday, and this meant two things: first, Theo was expected to spend at least thirty minutes with Ike, and, second, that dinner would be Italian food at Robilio's. The visit to Robilio's was more pleasant than the visit with Ike.

"Yes, ma'am," he said as he placed her documents in his backpack. "I'll see you at Robilio's."

"Yes, dear, at seven."

"Got it," he said, opening the back door. He explained to Judge that he would be back in a few minutes.

Dinner was always at seven. When they ate at home, which was rare because his mother didn't enjoy cooking, they ate at seven. When they went out, they ate at seven. When they were on vacation, seven. When they visited friends they couldn't be so rude as to suggest a time for dinner, but since all their friends knew how important seven was to the Boone family, they usually accommodated them. Occasionally, when Theo stayed over with a pal or went camping or was out of town for some reason, he took great delight in eating dinner before or after seven.

Five minutes later he parked his bike at a rack in front of the courthouse and locked the chain. Family Court was on the third floor, next door to Probate Court and down the hall from Criminal Court. There were a lot of other courts in the building—Traffic, Property, Small Claims, Drug, Animal, Civil, Bankruptcy, and probably one or two Theo had not yet discovered.

He hoped to find April, but she was not there. The courtroom was deserted. The hallways were empty.

He opened the glass door to the clerk's office and stepped inside. Jenny, the beautiful, was waiting. "Well, hello, Theo," she said with a big smile as she looked up from her computer at the long counter.

"Hello, Jenny," he said. She was very pretty and young and Theo was in love. He would marry Jenny tomorrow if he could, but his age and her husband complicated things. Plus, she was pregnant, and this bothered Theo, though he mentioned it to no one.

"These are from my mother," Theo said as he handed over the papers. Jenny took them, studied them for a moment, then said, "My, my, more divorces."

Theo just stared at her.

She stamped and scribbled and went about the process of officially recording the papers.

Theo just stared at her.

"Are you going to the trial tomorrow?" he asked, finally.

"I might slip down if I can get away. You?"

"Yes. Can't wait."

"Should be interesting, huh?"

Theo leaned in a little closer and said, "You think he's guilty?"

Jenny leaned even closer and glanced around as if their secrets were important. "I sure do. What about you?"

"Well, he's presumed to be innocent."

"You spend too much time hanging around the law office, Theo. I asked what you think, off the record, of course."

"I think he's guilty."

"We'll see, won't we?" She gave him a quick smile, then turned away to finish her business.

"Say, Jenny. That trial this morning, the Finnemore case, I guess it's over, right?"

She glanced around suspiciously, as if they were not supposed to be discussing an ongoing case. "Judge Sanford adjourned at four this afternoon, to be continued in the morning."

"Were you in the courtroom?"

"No. Why do you ask, Theo?"

"I go to school with April Finnemore. Her parents are divorcing. Just curious."

"I see," she said with a sad frown.

Theo just stared at her.

"Bye, Theo."

Down the hall, the courtroom was locked. A bailiff with no gun and a tight, faded uniform was near the main door. Theo knew all the bailiffs and this one, Deputy Gossett, was one of the grumpier ones. Mr. Boone had explained that the bailiffs are usually the older and slower policemen who are nearing the end of their careers. They are given new titles— "bailiffs"—and reassigned to the courthouse, where things are duller and safer than on the streets.

"Hello, Theo," Deputy Gossett said with no smile.

"Hi, Deputy Gossett."

"What brings you around here?"

"Just filing stuff for my parents."

"Is that all?"

"Yes, sir."

"You sure you're not snooping around here to see if the courtroom is ready for the big trial?"

"That, too."

"That's what I figured. We've had some traffic today. A television news crew just left. Should be interesting."

"Are you working tomorrow?"

"Of course I'm working tomorrow," Deputy Gossett said, and his chest puffed out a little, as if the trial would be impossible to put on without him. "Security will be tight."

"Why?" Theo asked, though he knew why. Deputy Gossett thought he knew a lot about the law, as if he'd absorbed a great body of knowledge just because he sat through trials and hearings. (He was often half asleep.) And, like many people who don't know as much as they think they know, Deputy Gossett was quick to share his insights with the less informed.

He glanced at his watch as if he had a tight schedule. "It's a murder trial, a big one," he said importantly. No kidding, Theo thought. "And, well, murder trials attract some folks who might be security risks."

"Like who?"

"Well, Theo, let me put it like this. In every murder there's a victim, and the victim has friends and family, and these people are, naturally, not happy that their victim got murdered. Follow what I'm saying?"

"Sure."

"And you have a defendant. In this case it's Mr. Duffy, who claims he's not guilty. They all say that, of course, but let's assume he's not guilty. If that's the case, then the real killer is still out there. He might be curious about the trial." Deputy Gossett glanced around suspiciously, as if the real killer could be close and might be offended.

Theo almost asked: Why would the real killer be a security risk if he showed up to watch the trial? What's he gonna do? Kill somebody else? In open court? In front of dozens of witnesses?

"I see," Theo said. "You guys better be careful."

"We'll have things under control."

"I'll see you in the morning."

"You'll be here?"

"Sure."

Deputy Gossett was shaking his head. "I don't think so, Theo. This place will be packed. You won't find a seat."

"Oh, I talked to Judge Gantry this morning. He promised to save me great seats." Theo was walking away.

Deputy Gossett could not think of a response.

Ike was Theo's uncle, the older brother of Woods Boone. Before Theo was born, Ike had started the firm of Boone & Boone with Theo's parents. He had been a tax lawyer, one of the few in town. According to the scant information Theo could get on the subject, the three lawyers had enjoyed a pleasant and productive relationship until Ike did something wrong. Bad wrong. So wrong that he was stripped of his license to practice law. On several occasions Theo had asked his parents what, exactly, Ike did wrong, but his parents refused to give the details. They said they didn't want to talk about it. Or, that they would explain things when Theo was old enough to understand.

Ike was still doing tax work, but of a lesser variety. He was not a lawyer and not an accountant. But since he had to do something for a living, he prepared tax returns for working people and small businesses. His office was on the second floor of an old building downtown. A Greek couple ran a deli on the first floor. Ike did their tax work and was paid in part with a free lunch five days a week.

His wife divorced him after he was disbarred. He was lonely and generally unpleasant, and Theo did not always enjoy stopping by every Monday afternoon. But Ike was family and that mattered, according to Theo's parents, though they spent almost no time with him.

"Hello, Theo," Ike called out as Theo opened the door to a long, cluttered room and stepped inside.

"Hello, Ike." Though he was older than Theo's father, he insisted on being called Ike. Like Elsa, it was part of his effort to stay young. He wore faded jeans, sandals, a T-shirt that advertised beer, and various beaded bracelets on his left wrist. His hair was long, wild, white, and gathered in the back in a ponytail.

Ike was at his desk, a wide table stacked with files. The Grateful Dead played softly on a stereo. Cheap funky art covered the walls.

According to Mrs. Boone, Ike had been the typical dark-suited, buttoned-up corporate tax man before he got into trouble. Now he fancied himself as an old hippie, anti-everything. A real rebel.

"How's my favorite nephew?" he asked as Theo settled into a chair across the desk.

"Great." Theo was the only nephew. "How was your day?"

Ike waved at the debris littering his desk and said, "The usual. Just sorting out the money problems of people with no money. How are things over at Boone and Boone?"

"The same." Though he was only four blocks away, Ike seldom saw Theo's parents. They were somewhat friendly, but the past was complicated.

"How's school going?"

"Fine."

"Straight A's?"

"Yes. Maybe an A minus in Chemistry."

"I expect straight A's."

You and everyone else, Theo thought. He wasn't sure how or why Ike thought he was entitled to an opinion about Theo's grades, but he figured that's what uncles were for. According to his parents, Ike was brilliant and had finished college in just three years.

"Your mother is well?"

"Mom's great, working hard." Ike never asked about Mr. Boone.

"I suppose you're excited about the trial tomorrow."

"Yes. My Government class is taking a field trip to the courtroom. We'll be there all day. Are you going?" Theo asked, but he knew the answer.

Ike snorted in disgust. "Not me. I don't voluntarily enter courtrooms. Plus, I have too much work." A typical Boone.

"I can't wait," Theo said.

"So you still want to be a lawyer, a great trial lawyer?"

"What's wrong with that?"

"Oh, nothing, I guess." They had this same conversation every week. Ike wanted Theo to be an architect or an artist, something creative. "Most kids dream of being a policeman, or a fireman, or a great athlete or actor. I've never seen one so taken with the idea of being a lawyer."

"Everybody's gotta be something."

"I suppose. This defense lawyer, Clifford Nance, is very good. You ever seen him in action?"

"Not in a big trial. I've seen him in the courtroom arguing motions and stuff, but not in a trial."

"I knew Clifford well, at one point. Many years ago. I'll bet he wins."

"You really think so?"

"Sure. The prosecution has a weak case, from what I hear." Though he kept to himself, Ike had a knack for hearing the courthouse rumors. Theo's father suspected that Ike's information came from his weekly poker games with a group of retired lawyers.

"There's really no proof that Mr. Duffy killed his wife," Ike said. "The prosecutor might be able to establish a strong motive and arouse some suspicions, but nothing else."

"What's the motive?" Theo asked, though he thought he knew the answer. He wanted to see how much Ike knew, or how much he was willing to tell.

"Money. A million dollars. Mr. Duffy bought a million-dollar life insurance policy on his wife two years ago. In the event of her death, he gets a million dollars. His business was not doing well. He needed some cash, so the theory is that he, literally, took matters into his own hands."

"He choked her?" Theo had read every newspaper story about the murder and knew the cause of death.

"That's the theory. She died of strangulation. The prosecutor will claim that Mr. Duffy choked her, then ransacked the house, took her jewelry, tried to make it look as if she walked in on a burglar."

"What will Mr. Nance try and prove?"

"He doesn't have to prove anything, but he'll argue that there's no proof, no evidence that Mr. Duffy was at the scene of the crime. To my knowledge there are no witnesses who can place him there. It's a very tough case for the prosecution."

"Do you think he's guilty?"

Ike cracked at least eight knuckles and locked his hands behind his head. He thought for a moment, then said, "Probably. I'll bet Duffy planned it all very carefully, and that it went down exactly as he wanted it to. Those people do some strange things out there."

"Those people" were the residents of Waverly Creek, a wealthy community built around a twenty-seven-hole golf course and protected by gates. They were the newer residents, as opposed to the more established ones who lived in the town proper and considered themselves the real citizens of Strattenburg. The phrase "They live out at The Creek" was heard often and usually described people who added little to the community and were much too concerned with money. The divide made little sense to Theo. He had friends who lived out there. His parents had clients from Waverly Creek. It was only two miles east of the city, but it was often treated as if it belonged on another planet.

Mrs. Boone said that people in small towns spend too much time looking up to or down on others. She had lectured Theo since he was a small boy on the evils of judging people.

The conversation drifted to baseball, and, of course, the Yankees. Ike was a rabid Yankees fan and loved to spout statistics on all his favorite players. Though it was April, he was already predicting another World Series win. Theo argued as usual, but as a Twins fan he had little ammunition.

After thirty minutes, he left with the promise to stop by next week.

"Get that Chemistry grade up," Ike said sternly.

CHAPTER 5

Judge Henry Gantry tugged on the right sleeve of his long black robe to adjust it properly, then stepped through the massive oak door behind the bench of his courtroom. A bailiff suddenly yelled, "All rise for the Court!"

Everyone—spectators, jurors, lawyers, clerks, all the participants in the trial—bolted to their feet in one scramble. As Judge Gantry was establishing himself in his thronelike chair, the bailiff quickly rattled off his standard call to order: "Hear ye, hear ye, the Criminal Court of the Tenth District is now in session, the Honorable Henry Gantry presiding. Let all who have matters come forth. May God bless this Court."

"Please be seated," Judge Gantry said loudly into the

microphone before him. Just as suddenly as the crowd had jumped to its feet, it fell backward in one collective motion. Chairs squeaked. Benches cracked. Purses and briefcases were rearranged, and the two hundred or so people all seemed to exhale at once. Then everything was quiet.

Judge Gantry quickly surveyed the courtroom. As expected, it was filled to capacity. "Well, we certainly have a lot of interest today," he said. "Thank you for your presence." He glanced up at the balcony, made eye contact with Theo Boone, then smiled at the presence of his classmates sitting shoulder to shoulder, all frozen at attention.

"The matter at hand is the case of the State versus Mr. Peter Duffy. Is the State ready to proceed?"

Jack Hogan, the prosecutor, stood and announced, "Yes, Your Honor, the State is ready."

"Is the defense ready to proceed?"

Clifford Nance rose and solemnly said, "We are ready, Your Honor."

Judge Gantry turned to his right, looked at his jury, and said, "Now, ladies and gentlemen of the jury, you were selected last week, and when you left here I gave you specific instructions not to discuss this case with anyone. I warned you that if anyone tried to approach you and discuss the case, then you were to notify me. I now ask if that has happened. Any contact from anyone about this case?"

All jurors shook their heads in the negative.

"Good. We have disposed of all pretrial motions, and we are now ready to begin. At this stage of the trial, both sides will have the opportunity to address you directly and make what we refer to as opening statements. An opening statement is not proof, not evidence, just a summary of each side's version of what happened. Since the State has the burden of proving guilt, the State will always go first. Mr. Hogan, are you ready?"

"Yes, sir."

"You may proceed."

Theo had been unable to eat breakfast, and he'd slept little. He'd read many stories of athletes who were so nervous they couldn't eat or sleep before a big game. They were overcome with butterflies, queasy stomachs brought on by fear and pressure. Theo could certainly feel the pressure right now. The air in the courtroom was heavy and tense. Though he was only a spectator, he had the butterflies. This was the big game.

Mr. Hogan was a career prosecutor who handled the major cases in Strattenburg. He was tall, wiry, bald, and wore a black suit every day. Behind his back folks joked about his black suits. No one knew if he had only one or a couple dozen. Though he rarely smiled, he began his opening statement with a friendly "good morning" and introduced himself and the two younger prosecutors at his table. He did a nice job of breaking the ice.

Then he got down to business. He introduced the victim, Myra Duffy, by showing the jury a large color portrait of her. "She was only forty-six years old when she was murdered," he said gravely. "The mother of two sons, Will and Clark, both college students. I'd like for them to stand." He pointed to the front row, directly behind the prosecution's table, and the two young men stood awkwardly and looked at the jurors.

Theo knew from the newspaper reports that their father, her first husband, had been killed in a plane crash when they were little boys. Mr. Duffy was her second husband, and she was his second wife.

People liked to say that there was a lot of remarrying "out at The Creek."

Mr. Hogan was describing the crime. Mrs. Duffy had been found in the living room of the large contemporary home she shared with Mr. Duffy. It was a new home, less than three years old, and it was on a wooded lot that backed up to the golf course. Because of all the trees, the house was barely visible from the street, but then the same could be said of most of the homes at Waverly Creek. Privacy was important out there.

When her body was found, the front door of their home was unlocked and slightly open. The alarm system was in Standby mode. Someone had taken her jewelry from her closet, a set of antique watches owned by Mr. Duffy, and three handguns from a drawer by the television in the den. The estimated value of the missing loot was about thirty thousand dollars.

The cause of death was strangulation. With the approval of Judge Gantry, Mr. Hogan stepped to a projector, hit a button, and a large color photo appeared on a screen opposite the jury. It showed Mrs. Duffy lying on the carpeted floor, well dressed, seemingly untouched, her high-heeled shoes still on her feet. Mr. Hogan explained that on the day she was murdered, a Thursday, she'd had a luncheon date at noon with her sister. Apparently, she was ready to leave the house when she was attacked and killed. Her murderer then went through the house, took the items that were missing, and left. Her sister began calling Mrs. Duffy's cell phone, ten calls over the next two hours, and became concerned enough that she drove to Waverly Creek, to the Duffy home, and found her sister. As far as crime scenes go, this one looked rather peaceful. The victim could've simply fainted. At first, her sister and the police thought she had died of a heart attack or a stroke or some other natural cause. But given her age, fitness, and no history of drug abuse, they quickly became suspicious.

An autopsy revealed the true cause of death. The person who killed Mrs. Duffy grabbed her from behind and pressed firmly on her carotid artery. Mr. Hogan placed his fingers against his own carotid artery, on the right side of his neck. "Ten seconds of firm pressure in just the right place and you lose consciousness," he said, then waited while everyone else waited to see if he might just collapse himself right there in open court. He did not. He continued, "Once Mrs. Duffy passed out, her killer kept pressing, firmer and firmer, and sixty seconds later she was dead. There are no signs of struggle—no broken fingernails, no scratches, nothing. Why? Because Mrs. Duffy knew the man who killed her."

Mr. Hogan dramatically turned and glared at Mr. Duffy, who was seated between Clifford Nance and another defense lawyer.

"She knew him because she was married to him."

There was a long, heavy pause as the entire courtroom looked at Mr. Duffy. Theo could see the back of his head. He wanted desperately to see his face.

Mr. Hogan continued, "He was able to get so close because she trusted him."

Mr. Hogan stood by the projector and displayed more

photographs. Using them, he laid out the entire scene—the interior of the house, the front door, the rear door, the close proximity to the golf course. He used a photo of the main entrance of Waverly Creek, with its heavy gates and guardhouse and security cameras. He explained that it was highly unlikely that an intruder, even a clever one, could breach all that security. Unless, of course, the intruder was not really an intruder because he lived there, too.

None of the neighbors saw a strange vehicle leave the Duffy home. No one saw a stranger walking the streets, or running from the house. Nothing unusual was reported. In the past six years, there had been only two home burglaries at Waverly Creek. Crime was virtually unheard of in this quiet community.

On the day of the murder, Mr. Duffy played golf, something he did almost every Thursday. He teed off at 11:10 a.m., according to the computer log in the golf shop. He was alone, which was not unusual, and, as always, he used his own electric golf cart. He told the course starter that he planned to play eighteen holes, the North Nine and the South Nine, the two most popular courses. The Duffy home bordered the sixth fairway of the Creek Course, a smaller course preferred by the ladies.

Mr. Duffy was a serious golfer who always kept score and didn't cheat. Playing eighteen holes alone usually took about three hours. The day was overcast, cool, and windy—weather that would discourage most people from playing golf. Other than a foursome that had teed off at ten twenty, there was no one else on any of the three courses at eleven ten. Another foursome teed off at one forty.

Mrs. Duffy's sister found her and immediately called 911. The call was recorded at 2:14 p.m. The autopsy placed her time of death at around eleven forty-five.

With the help of an assistant, Mr. Hogan set up a large diagram of the Waverly Creek community. He identified the three golf courses, the golf shop, driving range, tennis courts, and other points of interest, then he showed the jury the location of the Duffy home on the Creek Course. According to tests the State had performed, Mr. Duffy was either on the fourth or fifth hole of the North Nine at the time of his wife's murder. Riding in a golf cart identical to the one owned by Mr. Duffy, a person could travel from that part of the course to the Duffy home on the sixth fairway in about eight minutes.

Peter Duffy looked at the diagram and slowly shook his head as if Mr. Hogan was full of nonsense. He was forty-nine years old with a dark, scowling face topped by thick, graying hair. He wore horn-rimmed glasses, a brown suit, and could easily have been mistaken for one of the lawyers.

Jack Hogan drove home the point that Mr. Duffy knew

his wife was home, obviously had access to his own house, was in a golf cart only minutes away at the time of the murder, and was playing golf at a time when the course was practically deserted. His chances of being seen were slim.

"He planned it very well," Mr. Hogan said, over and over.

The mere fact that a good lawyer kept saying that Mr. Duffy killed his wife made his theory sound believable. Repeat something enough and folks will start to believe it. Mr. Mount had always taken the position that the presumption of innocence is a joke nowadays. The presumption is one of guilt. And, Theo had to admit, it was difficult to think of Mr. Duffy in terms of innocence, at least in the opening minutes of the trial.

Why would Mr. Duffy kill his wife? Mr. Hogan posed this question to the jury in such a way that it was obvious he had the answer.

"Money, ladies and gentlemen." With great drama, he snatched a document from his table and announced, "This is a life insurance policy for one million dollars purchased by Mr. Peter Duffy two years ago insuring the life of his late wife, Myra Duffy."

Dead silence. The guilt seemed to grow heavier.

Mr. Hogan flipped through the policy as he discussed

it, and seemed to lose some steam. When he was finished with it, he tossed it back on his table, then launched into a rambling discussion of Mr. Duffy's business woes. He was a real estate developer who had scored big, lost big, and at the time of his wife's death was being squeezed by some banks. Mr. Hogan promised the jury that the State would prove that the defendant, Peter Duffy, was on the verge of going broke.

Thus, he needed cash. As in life insurance money.

There was more on the subject of motive. Mr. Hogan said that the jury would learn that the Duffy marriage had not been a happy one. There had been problems, and lots of them. They had separated on at least two occasions. Both had hired divorce lawyers, though neither had ever filed for divorce.

To wrap things up, Mr. Hogan stood as close as possible to the jurors and gave them a serious look. "This was a cold-blooded murder, ladies and gentlemen. Perfectly planned and carefully executed. Not a hitch. No witnesses, no evidence left behind. Nothing but a lovely young woman brutally choked to death." Mr. Hogan suddenly closed his eyes, tapped the side of his head, said, "Oh, I forgot something. I forgot to tell you that two years ago when Mr. Duffy bought the life insurance policy, he also began playing golf alone. He'd seldom played alone before then, and we'll bring in witnesses to prove it. Isn't that a coincidence? He planned this for two years. Quietly fitting his golf game around his wife's schedule, just waiting. Waiting for a cold and windy day so the course would be empty. Waiting for the perfect moment to sprint home, park his cart next to the patio, hustle through the back door, "Hi, honey, I'm home," then grab her when she wasn't looking. One minute later, she's dead. He'd planned this for so long, he knew just what to do. He grabbed her jewelry, grabbed his expensive watches, and grabbed the guns so the police would think it was the work of a burglar. Seconds later he was out the door, back in the golf cart flying along the fairways to number five on the North Nine, where he took a four iron, casually hit a nice shot, and finished another lonely game of golf."

Mr. Hogan paused. All was silent. He picked up his legal pad and returned to his seat. Ninety minutes had passed. Judge Gantry rapped his gavel and said, "Let's take a ten-minute recess."

Mr. Mount gathered his class at the end of a narrow hallway on the second floor. The boys were chatting excitedly about the drama they'd just witnessed. "This is much better than television," one said.

"All right," Mr. Mount said, "you've heard only one

side of the case. Just for fun, though, how many think he's guilty?"

At least a dozen hands shot up. Theo wanted to vote yes for guilt, but he knew it was premature.

"What about the presumption of innocence?" Mr. Mount asked.

"He did it," said Darren, the drummer. Several others voiced their agreement.

"He's guilty," said Brian, the swimmer.

"There's no way he's getting off."

"He planned it perfectly."

"He did it."

"Okay, okay," said Mr. Mount. "We're going to have this same conversation during the lunch break, after you've heard the other side."

The other side began with a bang. Clifford Nance waited until the courtroom was quiet before he walked to the jury box. He was about sixty with gray hair over his ears, a thick chest and arms, and a swagger that seemed to say that he'd never backed down from a fight, in court or out.

"Not a shred of evidence!" he boomed in a deep, husky voice that echoed off the walls.

"Not a shred of evidence!" he boomed again, as if

someone could have missed it the first time. Theo caught himself flinching.

"Nothing! No witnesses. No crime-scene proof. Nothing but this clean, neat, tidy little story Mr. Hogan has just shared with you, not one word of which is evidence. Just his fanciful version of what *maybe* could have happened. Maybe Pete Duffy wanted to kill his wife. Maybe he carefully planned it all. Maybe he raced around an empty golf course. Maybe he arrived at his home just in time to pull off one of the cleanest killings in history. Then, maybe he stole some things, left the front door open, raced away back to the fifth tee, and resumed his game. Maybe that's what happened."

Mr. Nance was pacing now, slowly, before the jury, a perfect rhythm to his words.

"Mr. Hogan is asking you, ladies and gentlemen, to play the Maybe Game. Maybe this happened, maybe that happened. And he wants you to play along because he has no proof. He has nothing. Nothing but a man playing golf, alone, minding his own business, while his wife gets murdered in their lovely home less than a mile away."

He stopped pacing and walked closer to the jurors. He picked out an elderly gentleman on the front row and seemed ready to pat him on the knee. He lowered his voice and said, "I don't really blame Mr. Hogan for playing the

Maybe Game. He really has no choice, and this is because he has no evidence. He has nothing but a vivid imagination."

Mr. Nance shuffled to his right and made eye contact with a middle-aged housewife. "Our Constitution, our laws, our rules of procedure, they're all built on the ideas of fairness. And guess what? There is absolutely no room for a bunch of 'maybes.' Our laws are clear. Judge Gantry will explain them later, and when he does, please listen carefully. You will not hear him utter the word *maybe* a single time. What you will hear is the very well-known and time-honored and old-fashioned American rule that says when the State accuses you of a crime, the State must walk in here with all of its resources—investigators, police, experts, prosecutors, crime-scene analysts, all of these smart and experienced people—and prove beyond a reasonable doubt that you did, in fact, commit the crime."

Mr. Nance shuffled to his left and looked sincerely, and convincingly, at the six jurors on the second row. He spoke with no notes, his words smooth, almost effortless, as though he'd done this a thousand times but had lost none of his passion.

"Beyond a reasonable doubt. Beyond a reasonable doubt. The State has a heavy burden, one that it cannot possibly meet."

He paused while everyone took a breath. He walked to the defense table, picked up a yellow legal pad, but did not look at it. He was an actor on center stage, and he knew his lines by heart. He cleared his voice, then at full volume continued. "Now, the law says that Pete Duffy does not have to testify, does not have to call witnesses in his defense, does not have to prove anything. And why is this? Well, it's very simple. He is protected by one of our most cherished safeguards. It's called the presumption of innocence." Mr. Nance turned and pointed at his client. "Pete Duffy sits here an innocent man, same as you, same as me."

He began pacing again, slowly, his eyes never leaving the eyes of the jurors. "However, Pete Duffy will testify. He wants to testify. He can't wait to testify. And when he takes that seat right here, on the witness stand, he will testify, under oath, and he will tell you the truth. The truth, ladies and gentlemen, is something far different from the little story Mr. Hogan just created. The truth, ladies and gentlemen, is that Pete Duffy was indeed playing golf that fateful day, and he was alone, his preferred way of playing. The records will reflect that he teed off at eleven ten, drove away from the first tee in his own golf cart, one that he keeps in his garage, as do most of his neighbors. He was on the course, alone, while his wife was at home getting ready to leave for a lunch in town. A thief, some unknown criminal who's still at large and will probably remain so at the rate we're going, entered the house quietly, and mistakenly thought no one was home. The alarm was off. The front door was unlocked, as was the back door. This was not, is still not, uncommon in this neighborhood. Unexpectedly, the thief encountered Myra Duffy, attacked her with his hands because he had no weapon, and at that point he became something else. He became a murderer."

Mr. Nance paused and walked to the defense table, where he picked up a glass of water and took a long drink. Everyone watched him. There was nothing else to watch.

"And he's still out there!" he said suddenly, practically yelling. "Or he could be here," he said, waving his arms, taking in the entire courtroom. "Since we're playing the Maybe Game, then maybe he's here, watching this trial. Why not? He's certainly safe from Mr. Hogan and his gang."

Theo noticed that several of the jurors glanced toward the spectators.

Mr. Nance shifted gears and talked about the life insurance policy, and specifically the fact that Mr. Duffy had indeed purchased one that made him the recipient of a million dollars in the event his wife died. But, there had been an identical policy on his life naming Mrs. Duffy as the recipient. They had simply done what most married couples do. They had purchased dual policies. He promised to prove to the jury that Pete Duffy's business affairs were not nearly as dire as Mr. Hogan claimed. He admitted that the Duffys had struggled with their marriage, and they had separated on more than one occasion, but they had never filed for divorce. In fact, they were determined to work through their differences.

Mr. Mount sat in the second row in the balcony, behind his students. He chose his spot carefully so he could see all sixteen, if necessary. So far they had been riveted by the opening statements. Not surprisingly, Theo was more engaged than the others. He was exactly where he wanted to be.

When Mr. Nance finished, Judge Gantry called for an early lunch recess.

CHAPTER 6

The Government class crossed Main Street and headed east, toward the river. Mr. Mount held back a step or two and listened with amusement as the boys argued back and forth, some of them using phrases and words they'd just heard from the real lawyers.

"This way," he said, and the group hung a left onto a narrow side street. They filed into Pappy's, a famous deli known for its pastrami subs and onion rings. It was ten minutes before noon and they had beaten the rush. They ordered quickly, then huddled around a long table near the front window.

"Who was the better lawyer?" Mr. Mount asked.

At least ten answered at once and there was an even split between Jack Hogan and Clifford Nance. Mr. Mount prodded them with questions like: "Which lawyer did you believe? Which would you trust? Which did the jury tend to follow?"

The food arrived and the conversation dropped dramatically.

"A show of hands," Mr. Mount said. "And you must vote. No fence straddling. Raise your hand if you think Mr. Duffy is guilty."

He counted ten hands. "Okay, not guilty."

He counted five hands. "Theo, I said you must vote."

"Sorry, but I can't vote. I think he's guilty, but I don't see how the State can prove its case. All they can prove is motive, maybe."

"The Maybe Game, huh?" Mr. Mount said. "I thought that was very effective."

"I'm with Theo," Aaron said. "He sure looks guilty, but the prosecutor can't even place him at the scene of the crime. That's a problem, right?"

"A large problem, I'd say," Mr. Mount replied.

"What about the stolen jewelry and watches and guns?" Edward asked. "Did they find this stuff? It was never mentioned."

"Don't know, but then the opening statements are somewhat limited."

"They seemed pretty long to me."

"We'll find out when the witnesses are called," Theo added.

"Who's the first witness?" Chase asked.

"I haven't seen the witness list," Mr. Mount said. "But they usually start with the crime scene. It'll probably be one of the detectives."

"Cool."

"How late can we stay today, Mr. Mount?"

"We have to be back at school at three thirty."

"How late will the trial go?"

"Judge Gantry likes to work," Theo said. "At least until five."

"Can we come back tomorrow, Mr. Mount?"

"Afraid not. It's a one-day field trip. You do have other classes, you know. None as exciting as mine, but that's just my opinion."

The deli was suddenly packed and a line formed outside. Mr. Mount told his students to finish up. Pappy, the owner, was famous for barking at people who occupied tables long after they had finished eating.

They strolled along Main Street, which was busy now with people scurrying around on their lunch breaks. At a fountain, office workers ate and talked while soaking up the sun. Officer Peacock, the ancient traffic cop, directed traffic with his worn-out whistle and yellow gloves, and managed to prevent accidents, which was not always the case with Officer Peacock. Just ahead, a group of men in dark suits left a building and headed in the same direction as the students. Mr. Mount whispered loudly, "Look, men, it's Mr. Duffy and his lawyers."

The boys slowed for a second as the group of dark suits moved on in front of them. Pete Duffy, Clifford Nance, two other solemn-faced lawyers, and a fifth man Theo had not seen in the courtroom that morning, but one he knew well. His name was Omar Cheepe, and he was not a lawyer, though he was well known in legal circles. Mr. Cheepe was a former federal agent of some variety who now ran his own firm. He specialized in investigations and surveillance and other activities that lawyers needed from time to time. He and Mrs. Boone had once been involved in a nasty dispute in a divorce case, and Theo had heard Omar Cheepe described as "an armed thug," and a "man who enjoyed breaking the law." Theo, of course, was not supposed to hear such comments, but then he heard a lot around the office. He had never actually met Mr. Cheepe, but he'd seen him in court. The rumor was that if Omar Cheepe was working on the case, then someone had to be guilty.

Omar looked directly at Theo. He was thick, powerfully

built, with a large round head that he kept shaved. The man tried to look menacing, and he was successful.

He turned away and hurried after Duffy.

They walked down Main Street, the boys in a loose group, moving fast to keep up with the defendant and his team. Omar Cheepe's hulking frame protected Pete Duffy from the rear, as if someone might take a shot. Clifford Nance told a funny story, and the men had a good laugh.

Pete Duffy laughed the loudest. Guilty. Theo hated to believe this because not a single witness had testified. Plus, he liked to tell himself that he believed in the presumption of innocence.

Guilty, Theo said again, to himself. Why couldn't he follow the law, give Mr. Duffy the benefit of innocence? Why couldn't he do what good lawyers were supposed to do? This frustrated him as he followed along behind Mr. Duffy and his lawyers.

There was something missing in the case, and based on what had already been said in court, Theo suspected that the mystery might never be solved.

They filed into their seats, front row left side of the balcony, and allowed their lunch to settle. Judge Gantry had recessed until 1:00 p.m., some fifteen minutes away.

Deputy Gossett, the old bailiff, lumbered over to them and said, "Theo."

"Yes, sir."

"Is this your class?"

What else would it be, Deputy Gossett? A teacher, sixteen students? "Yes, sir."

"Judge Gantry would like to see you, in chambers. And hurry. He's a busy man."

Theo pointed to himself, tried to think of something to say.

"The whole class," Deputy Gossett said. "And hurry."

They scrambled into formation behind Deputy Gossett and hustled down the stairs.

"In chambers" meant the judge was in his office behind the bench, adjacent to the courtroom. This office was different from his formal office down the hall. It was confusing and Theo was attempting to explain this when Deputy Gossett opened the door to a long, wood-paneled room with old portraits of old bearded judges covering the walls. Judge Gantry, without his black robe, rose from behind his desk and stepped out to meet the boys.

"Hello, Theo," he said, embarrassing Theo slightly. The other students were too awestruck to speak.

"And you must be Mr. Mount," the judge was saying as they shook hands.

"Yes, Judge, and this is my eighth-grade Government class."

Since there were not enough seats for everyone, Judge Gantry addressed the boys where they stood. "Thank you for coming. It's important for students to see our judicial system in action. What do you think so far?"

All sixteen boys were mute. What were they supposed to say?

Mr. Mount rescued them. "They are fascinated by the trial," he said. "We just debriefed over lunch, rated the lawyers, talked about the jurors, and had a lot of opinions about guilt and innocence."

"I won't ask. But we have a couple of pretty good lawyers, don't you think?"

All sixteen heads nodded.

"Is it true that Theo Boone actually gives legal advice?"

A few nervous laughs. Theo was both embarrassed and proud. "Yes, but I don't charge them anything," he said. A few more laughs.

"Any questions about the trial?" Judge Gantry asked.

"Yes, sir," Brandon said. "On television you always see a surprise witness that comes out of nowhere and changes the trial. Is there a chance of a surprise witness here? If not, it seems like the State has a pretty weak case."

"Good question, son. The answer is no. Our rules of

procedure prohibit surprise witnesses. Television gets it all wrong. In real life, before the trial starts, each side must provide a list of all potential witnesses."

"Who's the first witness?" Jarvis asked.

"The victim's sister, the lady who found the body. She'll be followed by the homicide detectives. How long can you stay today?"

"We need to be back at school at three thirty," Mr. Mount said.

"Okay. I'll call a recess at three, and you can ease out. How are the seats up in the balcony?"

"Great, and thank you."

"I've moved you down to the floor. Things have cleared out a bit. Again, thanks for taking such an interest in our judicial system. It's very important to good government." With that, Judge Gantry was finished. The students thanked him. He and Mr. Mount shook hands again.

Deputy Gossett led them out of chambers, back to the courtroom, down the main aisle, and to the second row behind the prosecution's table. In front of them were the two young men who'd been introduced as Mrs. Duffy's sons. The lawyers were only a few feet away. Across the aisle, Omar was now sitting behind Pete Duffy, his black eyes darting around the courtroom as if he might need to shoot someone. Once again, he looked directly at Theo.

They had gone from the cheap seats to ringside, and they couldn't believe it. Chase, the mad scientist, was to Theo's right, elbow to elbow. He whispered, "Did you pull some strings, Theo?"

"No, but Judge Gantry and I are pretty tight."

"Nice work."

At precisely 1:00 p.m., the bench bailiff stood and wailed, "Court is now in session. Please remain seated."

Judge Gantry appeared in his robe and took his seat. He looked at Jack Hogan and said, "The State may call its first witness."

From a side door, another bailiff escorted a well-dressed lady into the courtroom and to the witness chair. She placed her hand on a Bible and swore to tell the truth. When she was seated and the microphone adjusted, Mr. Hogan began his direct examination.

Her name was Emily Green, the sister of Myra Duffy. She was forty-four, lived in Strattenburg, worked as a fitness counselor, and on the day of the murder she had done exactly what Mr. Hogan described in his opening statement. When her sister didn't show for lunch, and didn't call, she became worried, then panicky. She called her repeatedly on her cell phone, then raced to Waverly Creek, to the Duffy home, and found her sister dead on the living room carpet.

It was obvious, at least to Theo, that Mr. Hogan and

Ms. Green had carefully rehearsed her testimony. It was designed to establish death, and to evoke sympathy. When they finished, Clifford Nance stood and announced that he had no questions on cross-examination. Ms. Green was excused, and she took a seat in the front row, next to her two nephews, directly in front of Mr. Mount's students.

The next witness was Detective Krone, from Homicide. Using the large screen and the projector, he and Jack Hogan laid out the neighborhood, the Duffy home, and the crime scene. Several important facts were established, though the jury already knew them. The front door was found open. The rear door and the side patio door were not locked. The alarm system was not engaged.

And new facts emerged. Fingerprint tests found matches throughout the house for Mr. Duffy, Mrs. Duffy, and their housekeeper, but this was to be expected. No other matches were found on doorknobs, windows, phones, drawers, the jewelry case, or the antique mahogany box where Mr. Duffy kept his expensive watches. This meant one of two things: (1) the thief/murderer wore gloves or carefully wiped away any prints, or (2) the thief/murderer was either Mr. Duffy or the housekeeper. The housekeeper was not at work on the day of the murder—she was out of town with her husband.

Whoever took the jewelry, guns, and watches had also yanked open several other cabinets and drawers and flung items on the floor. Detective Krone, who was pretty dull to listen to, methodically went through photo after photo of the mess left behind by the thief/murderer.

For the first time, the trial began to drag. Mr. Mount noticed a few of the boys starting to fidget. A couple of the jurors looked sleepy.

At precisely 3:00 p.m., Judge Gantry banged his gavel and announced a fifteen-minute recess. The courtroom emptied quickly. Everyone needed a break. Theo and his friends left the courthouse, boarded a small yellow bus, and ten minutes later were back at school in time for dismissal.

Thirty minutes after he left, Theo was back in the courthouse. He sprinted up the stairs to the third floor. There was no sign of the Finnemore war—no lawyers in the hallway, no sign of April. She had not called or answered his e-mails the night before, nor had she posted anything on her Facebook page. Her parents would not allow her to have a cell phone, so she could not text. This was not that unusual. About half of the eighth graders at the middle school did not have cell phones.

Theo hurried down to the second floor, entered the courtroom under the suspicious gaze of Deputy Gossett, and found a seat on the third row, behind the defense table. The defendant, Mr. Duffy, sat less than twenty feet away. Theo could hear his lawyers as they whispered important things. Omar Cheepe was still there. He noticed Theo when he sat down. As an experienced observer, Omar had the ability to see all movements, but he did it casually, as if he really didn't care.

The witness was a doctor, the medical examiner who performed the autopsy on the victim. He was using a large color diagram of a human body from the chest up, with emphasis on the neck area. Theo paid more attention to Clifford Nance than to the witness. He watched Mr. Nance as he listened intently to the testimony, and took notes, and continually glanced at the jury. He seemed to miss nothing in the courtroom. He was relaxed and confident, though ready to attack if necessary.

His cross-examination of the doctor was quick and revealed nothing new. So far, Mr. Nance seemed content to agree with most of the prosecution's witnesses. The fireworks would come later.

Judge Gantry adjourned court just after 5:00 p.m. Before he excused the jurors, he again warned them against discussing the case with anyone. After they filed out, the courtroom emptied. Theo hung around, watching the lawyers gather their files and books as they repacked their thick briefcases and talked in hushed tones. There were words across the aisle. Jack Hogan said something to Clifford Nance and both men laughed. The other, lesser lawyers joined in, and someone said, "How about a drink?"

Enemies one moment, old pals the next. Theo had seen it before. His mother had tried to explain that lawyers are paid to do a job, and to do it properly they had to park their personal feelings at the door. The real professionals, she said, never lose their cool and carry grudges.

Ike said that was nonsense. He despised most of the lawyers in town.

Omar Cheepe was not laughing, and he was not invited to have a drink with the enemy. He and Pete Duffy made a quick exit through a side door.

CHAPTER
7

Tuesday night meant dinner in a soup kitchen. It wasn't the worst meal of the week. That would be Sunday night, when his mother attempted to roast a chicken. But it wasn't a great meal either.

The soup kitchen was just called that. It really wasn't a kitchen and they rarely served soup. It was a large dining room in the basement of a converted church where homeless people gathered to eat and spend the night. The food was prepared by volunteers who usually offered sandwiches, chips, fruit, cookies.

"Stuff from a bag," Theo's mother called it. Not all that healthy.

Theo had heard that there were around three hundred homeless people in Strattenburg. He saw them on Main Street, where they begged for money and slept on benches. He saw them in garbage Dumpsters scrounging for food. The city was alarmed at this number and by the lack of beds in shelters. The city council seemed to argue about this problem every week.

Mrs. Boone was alarmed, too. She had been so concerned about homeless mothers that she started a program to assist victims of domestic violence. Women who'd been beaten and threatened. Women who had no place to live, no one to turn to. Women with children who needed help and didn't know where to find it. Mrs. Boone, along with several of the other female lawyers in town, had started a small legal clinic to reach out to these women.

And so every Tuesday night, the Boone family walked a few blocks from their office downtown to the Highland Street Shelter, where they spent three hours with the less fortunate. They took their turns serving dinner to the hundred or so folks gathered there, then afterward they had a quick bite.

Though he wasn't supposed to know, Theo had overheard his parents discussing whether they should increase their monthly donation to the shelter from two hundred to three hundred dollars. His parents were far from wealthy. His friends thought he was rich because both parents were lawyers, but the truth was their work was not that profitable. They lived modestly, saved for Theo's education, and enjoyed being generous with those of lesser means.

After dinner, Mr. Boone set up a makeshift office at the far end of the dining room, and a few homeless people drifted that way. He would help them with problems that usually ranged from being evicted from their apartments to being denied food stamps or medical care. He often said that these were his favorite clients. They couldn't pay a fee, so there was no pressure to collect from them. They were grateful for whatever he tried to do. And, he genuinely enjoyed talking to them.

Because of the more sensitive nature of her work, Mrs. Boone saw her clients in a small room upstairs. The first client had two small children, no job, no money, and, if not for the shelter, no place to sleep that night.

Theo's task was to help with the homework. The shelter had several families that were allowed to stay there for up to twelve months—that was the limit at Highland Street. After a year, they had to move on. Most of them found jobs and places to live, but it took time. While they were in the shelter, they were treated like other residents of Strattenburg. They were fed and clothed and treated for medical problems. They were either employed or looking for work. They were invited to churches for worship.

And their children attended the local schools. At night, in the shelter, homework sessions were organized by volunteers from a church. Theo's job every Tuesday was to teach English to two second graders, Hector and Rita, and to help their brother with algebra. They were from El Salvador, and their father had disappeared under mysterious circumstances, leaving them homeless. They were found by the police living under a bridge with their mother.

As always, Hector and Rita were thrilled to see Theo and clung to him as he stuffed down his sandwich. Then they scurried down the hall to a large open room where other children were being tutored.

"No Spanish," he said repeatedly. "Only English."

Their English was amazing. They were absorbing it daily at school and teaching it to their mother. They found a corner table and Theo began reading a picture book, something about a frog lost at sea.

Mrs. Boone had insisted that Theo start Spanish in the fourth grade, as soon as it was offered. When the classes proved too easy, she hired a private tutor who stopped by the office twice a week for rigorous lessons. With his mother pushing him hard, and with Madame Monique giving him daily inspiration, Theo was learning rapidly.

He read a page, then Rita reread it. Then Hector. Theo corrected their mistakes, then moved on. The room was noisy, even rowdy, as two dozen or so students of all ages plowed through their homework.

The twins had an older brother, Julio, a seventh grader Theo saw occasionally on the playground at school. He was extremely shy, to the point of being awkward. Mrs. Boone speculated that the poor kid was probably scarred from the trauma of losing his father in a strange country with no one to turn to.

She always had a theory when someone acted strange.

After Theo finished the second book with Hector and Rita, Julio joined them and sat down at the table.

"What's up?" Theo said.

Julio smiled and looked away.

"Let's read another book," Hector said.

"In a minute."

"I'm having trouble with algebra," Julio said. "Can you help?"

"He's with us," Rita said to her brother, and appeared ready to fight.

Theo picked out two books from a shelf and placed

them before Hector and Rita. Then he arranged two writing tablets and two pencils. "Read these books," he said. "Say every word as you read it. When you see a word you don't know, write it down. Okay?"

They yanked the books open as if it were a contest.

Theo and Julio were soon lost in the world of pre-algebra.

At 10:00 p.m., the Boones were at home in front of the television. Judge was asleep on the sofa, his head in Theo's lap. The Duffy murder was the only news in Strattenburg and the town's two television stations covered nothing else that evening. There was a video of Pete Duffy walking into the courthouse, surrounded by lawyers and paralegals and other men with dark suits and somber faces. Another video, this one shot from the air, showed the Duffy home on the sixth fairway at Waverly Creek. A reporter outside the courthouse gave a rapid-fire account of the testimony so far. Judge Gantry had a gag order in place; thus, none of the lawyers or police or other witnesses could share their thoughts or opinions.

Judge Gantry also banned cameras from his courtroom. The news crews were kept out.

Theo had talked of nothing else, and his parents shared

his suspicion that Pete Duffy was guilty. Proving it, though, looked difficult.

During a commercial break, Theo began coughing. When this did not get the attention of his parents, he coughed some more, then said, "My throat is getting sore."

"You look sort of pale," his father said. "You must be getting sick."

"I don't feel well."

"Are your eyes red?" his father asked.

"I think so."

"A headache?"

"Yes, but not bad."

"Sniffles, runny nose?"

"Yes."

"When did this happen?" his mother asked.

"You're a very sick boy," his father said. "I say you should skip school tomorrow so you won't spread this terrible infection. But, it might be a good idea to go to court instead and watch the Duffy trial. What do you think, Mom?"

"Oh, I see," she said. "A sudden onset of the flu."

"Probably just another one of those nasty twenty-four-hour episodes that seems to end miraculously when the school day is over," his father said.

"I really don't feel well," Theo said, busted but gamely trying to hang on.

"Take an aspirin, maybe a cough drop," his father said. Woods Boone seldom saw a doctor and believed most people spent far too much money on medications.

"Can you cough again for us, Teddy?" his mother asked. As a mother, she was slightly more sympathetic when he felt bad. The truth was that Theo had a history of faking it, especially when he had something better to do than go to school.

His father started laughing. "Yes, it was a pretty lame cough, Theo, even by your standards."

"I could be dying," Theo said, trying not to laugh.

"Yes, but you're not," his father said. "And if you show up in the courtroom tomorrow Judge Gantry will have you arrested as a truant."

"You know any good lawyers?" Theo shot back. His mother burst out laughing, and, eventually, Woods saw the humor.

"Go to bed," he said.

Theo limped up the stairs, thoroughly defeated, with Judge trailing behind. In bed, he opened his laptop and checked on April. He was relieved when she answered,

APRILNPARIS: Hi, Theo. How are you?
TBOONEESQ: Okay. Where are you?

APRILNPARIS: At home, in my bedroom, with my
door locked.

TBOONEESQ: Where's your mother?

APRILNPARIS: Downstairs. We're not speaking.

TBOONEESQ: Did you make it to school?

APRILNPARIS: No, the trial lasted until noon. I'm so glad
it's over.

TBOONEESQ: How was it on the witness stand?

APRILNPARIS: Terrible. I cried, Theo. I couldn't stop
crying. I told the judge that I didn't want to live with my
mother or my father. Her lawyer asked me questions.
His lawyer asked me questions. It was awful.

TBOONEESQ: I'm sorry.

APRILNPARIS: I don't understand why you want to
be a lawyer.

TBOONEESQ: To help people like you, that's why. That's
what good lawyers do. Did you like the judge?

APRILNPARIS: I didn't like anybody.

TBOONEESQ: My mom says he's good. Did he make
a decision about your custody?

APRILNPARIS: No. He said he would in a few days.
For now, I'm living with my mother and her lawyer thinks
I'll stay here.

TBOONEESQ: Probably so. Will you be at school
tomorrow?

APRILNPARIS: Yep, and I haven't touched my
homework in a week.
TBOONEESQ: I'll see you tomorrow.
APRILNPARIS: Thanks, Theo.

An hour later he was still awake, his thoughts switching
back and forth, from April to the Duffy murder trial.

CHAPTER 8

Julio was waiting. Theo slid to a stop at the bike rack near the flagpole in front of the school and said, "*Hola*, Julio. *Buenós días.*"

"*Hola*, Theo."

Theo wrapped the chain around the front tire and clicked the lock. The chain still frustrated him. Up until a year earlier, bikes were safe in Strattenburg. No one bothered with a chain. Then bikes began disappearing, still were, and parents began insisting on the extra security.

"Thanks for your help last night," Julio said. His English was good, but still heavily accented. The fact that he had approached Theo at school and initiated a conversation was a big step forward. Or so Theo thought.

"No problem. Anytime."

Julio glanced around. A crowd from the buses was moving through the front door. "You know the law, right, Theo?"

"Both my parents are lawyers."

"Police, courts, all that?"

Theo shrugged. He never denied that he possessed a sizable knowledge of the law. "I understand a lot of it," he said. "What's up?"

"This big trial, is it Mr. Duffy?"

"Yes, he's on trial for murder. And it is a big trial."

"Can we talk about it?"

"Sure," Theo said. "May I ask why?"

"Maybe I know something."

Theo studied his eyes. Julio looked away, as if he'd done something wrong. An assistant principal yelled at some students to stop mingling and get inside. Theo and Julio headed for the door.

"I'll find you during lunch," Theo said.

"Good. Thanks."

"No problem."

As if Theo didn't have enough of the Duffy trial on his mind, now he had even more. A lot more. What could a homeless twelve-year-old from El Salvador possibly know about the murder of Myra Duffy?

Nothing, Theo decided as he walked to homeroom. He said good morning to Mr. Mount as he unpacked his backpack. He was not happy. The trial, the biggest trial in the history of Strattenburg, would start again in half an hour, and he would not be there. There is no justice, he decided.

During the morning recess, Theo sneaked away to the library and hid in a study carrel. He pulled out his laptop and went to work.

The court reporter assigned to the Duffy trial was a Ms. Finney. She was the best in town, according to what Theo had heard around the courthouse. As in every trial, Ms. Finney sat at the foot of the bench, below the judge and next to the witness chair. It was the best seat in the house, and rightfully so. Her job was to record every word spoken by the judge, the lawyers, the witnesses, and, finally, the jury. Using her stenograph machine, Ms. Finney could easily take down 250 words a minute.

In the old days, according to Mrs. Boone, the court reporters used shorthand, a method of recording that included symbols and codes and abbreviations and pretty much anything else they needed to keep up with the dialogue. After the trial, the court reporter would translate

to account for every nonresident who might have gone past the gates.

And to prove what? Maybe Jack Hogan would try to prove that there were no unauthorized vehicles, or people, in Waverly Creek at the time of the murder. This seemed a stretch to Theo.

He realized he was missing a dull part of the trial. He turned off his laptop and hustled to class.

.

Julio was not in the cafeteria. Theo ate in a hurry, then went to look for him. His curiosity was nagging him, and the longer he sat through class, the more he wanted to know what Julio *might* know. He checked with some seventh graders. No one knew where Julio was.

Theo returned to the library, to the same study carrel, and quickly hacked into Ms. Finney's software. The trial was in recess for lunch, as Theo expected. Otherwise, he would have found some excuse to dart downtown during the noon break and check out the action.

As expected, the prosecution had attempted to prove that there were no unauthorized vehicles in Waverly Creek at the time of the murder. Therefore, to follow Jack Hogan's theory, the killer was not someone who had entered without permission. Any stranger would have been noticed by the elaborate security. The killer, then, had to be someone who could easily come and go without drawing attention from the guards. Someone who lived there. Someone like Pete Duffy.

This effort by the prosecution drew heavy fire from Mr. Clifford Nance, who had kept quiet during the early hours of the trial. During a heated and sometimes harsh cross-examination, Mr. Nance forced the security chief to admit that there were (1) 154 single-family homes and 80 condos in Waverly Creek; and (2) at least 477 vehicles owned by the residents there; and (3) an asphalt service road that was not watched by either guards or cameras; and (4) at least two gravel roads that provided access to the area and were not on the map.

Mr. Nance drove home the point that Waverly Creek covered some twelve hundred acres, with lots of streams, creeks, ponds, woods, coves, streets, alleys, homes, condos, three golf courses, and, well, it was "impossible" to secure all that.

The chief reluctantly agreed.

Later, he admitted that it was impossible to know who was present inside the gated community at the time of the murder and who wasn't.

Theo thought the cross-examination was brilliant, and very effective. It made him sadder that he had missed it.

"What are you doing?" The voice startled Theo and snapped him back into the world of middle school. It was April. She knew his hiding places.

"Checking on the trial."

"I hope I never see another trial."

He closed his laptop, and they moved to a small table near the periodicals. She wanted to talk, and in a near whisper she replayed the nightmare of testifying in court with a bunch of frowning adults hanging on every word.

Final bell was at three thirty, and twenty minutes later Theo was in the courtroom. It wasn't as crowded as it had been the day before. Luckily, he found a spot next to Jenny, his true love from the Family Court clerk's office. But she patted his knee, as if he were just a cute little puppy. This always irritated Theo.

The jury was out. Judge Gantry was gone. The trial was in some sort of recess. "What's going on?" he whispered.

"The lawyers are haggling in chambers," she whispered back, frowning with frustration.

"You still think he's guilty?" His voice was even lower.

"Yes. You?"

"Don't know."

They whispered back and forth for a few minutes, then there was a flurry of movement up front. Judge Gantry was back. The lawyers were filing into the room. A bailiff went to fetch the jury.

The next witness for the prosecution was a banker. Jack Hogan started with a series of questions about loans made to Pete Duffy. There was a lot of talk about finances and collateral and defaults, and much of it was over Theo's head. As he watched the jurors, he realized that most of them were not following too well either. The testimony quickly became dull and boring. If it was intended to prove that Pete Duffy was broke and needed cash, then Theo thought the banker was a lousy witness.

It was a bad day for the prosecution, at least in his opinion. He glanced around the courtroom and realized that the sinister Omar Cheepe was not present. Theo figured he was close by, somewhere, watching or listening.

The banker was in the process of putting everyone to sleep. Theo glanced up and back at the balcony, which was empty except for one person. Julio was there. He was at the far end of the front row, bent at the waist, his head barely visible over the railing, as if he knew he wasn't supposed to be there.

Theo turned back around, looked at the witness and the jury, and asked himself why Julio would possibly be watching the trial.

He knew something.

A few minutes later, Theo glanced up again. Julio was not alone anymore. Omar Cheepe was sitting directly behind him, and Julio did not know he was being observed.

CHAPTER
9

Judge Gantry adjourned court shortly after 5:00 p.m and called the lawyers into his chambers for what promised to be a tense meeting. Theo hurried outside and looked for Julio, but there was no sign, no trail. A few minutes later, Theo parked behind the family's law office and went inside. Elsa was tidying up her desk, getting ready to leave.

"A good day at school, Theo?" she asked with her customary warm smile as she hugged him.

"No."

"And why not?"

"I'm bored with school."

"Of course. And school is especially boring when there's a trial under way, right?"

"Right."

"Your mother has a client. Your father was putting the last I heard."

"He needs the practice," Theo said. "Bye."

"Bye, dear. See you tomorrow." Elsa left through the front door and Theo locked it behind her.

Woods Boone kept a putter and a few balls near his desk. He practiced on an old Oriental rug that had very little in common with a real putting green. Several times a day, when he "needed to stretch his back" he would tap a few balls. When he missed, which was more often than not, the balls rolled off the rug and across the wooden floor and made a distinct sound, one that was not quite as loud as a bowling ball roaring down the alley, but a racket nonetheless. The entire firm downstairs knew that the errant golfer upstairs had missed once again.

"Well, hello, Theo," Mr. Boone said. He was at his desk, not putting, sleeves rolled up, pipe stuck between his right rear molars, a mountain of paperwork in front of him.

"Hey, Dad."

"A good day at school?"

"Great." If Theo complained, which he occasionally

couldn't help, then he would get the standard lecture about the importance of education and so on. "I stopped by the courthouse after school."

"I figured. Anything exciting?"

They talked about the trial for a few minutes. His father seemed to have almost no interest in it, and this baffled Theo. How could any lawyer not be consumed with such an important event in the town's judicial system?

The phone rang and Mr. Boone excused himself. Theo went downstairs to check on the rest of the firm. Vince the paralegal was working with his door shut. Dorothy the real estate assistant was gone. Theo heard serious voices coming from his mother's office, so he eased along the hall. He often heard people crying in there, women who were overwhelmed with marital problems and were in desperate need of his mother's help.

Theo couldn't help but smile at his mother's importance. He had no desire to be her type of lawyer, but he was very proud of her anyway.

He went to his office, spent a few minutes chatting with Judge, and started his homework. A few minutes dragged by and it was getting dark. Judge growled at a sound from the outside, then someone knocked on his door. Theo, startled, jumped to his feet and looked outside. It was Julio. Theo opened the door.

"Can we talk out here?" Julio said, nodding away from the building.

"Sure," Theo said, and pulled the door closed behind him. "What's up?"

"I don't know."

"I saw you in court a while ago. Why were you in court?"

Julio took a few steps away from the office, as if someone in there might hear him. He glanced around, very nervously. "I need to trust someone, Theo," he said. "Someone who knows the law."

"You can trust me," Theo said, quite anxious to hear the rest of a story he'd been thinking about the entire day.

"But if I tell you something, you cannot tell anyone else, okay?"

"Okay, but why would you tell me something if I can't tell anyone? I don't understand."

"I need advice. Someone needs to know."

"Know what?"

Julio stuck both hands in the pockets of his jeans. His shoulders dropped. He looked frightened. Theo thought about him, his mother, and his little brother and sister. Living in a shelter, far from their real home, abandoned by their father. They were probably afraid of almost everything.

"You can trust me, Julio," Theo said.

"Okay." Julio looked at his feet, unable to make eye contact. "I have a cousin, from El Salvador. He's here, in Strattenburg. He's older, maybe eighteen or nineteen. Been here a year or so. He works out at the golf course. He cuts grass, puts water in the coolers, all that sort of stuff. Do you play golf?"

"Yes."

"Then you see the guys who take care of the course."

"Yes." Theo played with his father every Saturday morning on the Strattenburg municipal course. There were always a few workers—mostly Hispanic, now that he thought of it—around the fairways and greens taking care of things.

"Which golf course?" Theo asked. There were at least three in the area.

"Out there, where the lady was murdered."

"Waverly Creek?"

"Yes."

Theo felt something tighten in his upper chest, a knot of some sort, one that had just formed. "Go on," he said, though something told him he should drop this conversation at once, run back into the office, and lock the door.

"You see, he was working on the day of the murder. He was eating lunch. His lunch break starts at eleven thirty and goes to twelve. He is very homesick, and on most days he sneaks away from the others and eats alone. He carries a family photo of his mother, father, and four little brothers, and while he eats he looks at the photo. It makes him very sad, but it also reminds him of why he's here. He sends them money every month. They are very poor."

"Where does he eat lunch?" Theo asked, but he already had a clue.

"I don't know much about golf, just what he has told me. Fairway and dogleg, you know these words?"

"Sure."

"Well, my cousin was sitting under some trees in a dogleg, sort of hiding because his lunch break is the only time he can be alone, and he saw this man in a golf cart going real fast down the path along the fairway. The man had a set of golf clubs on the back of the cart, but he was not hitting balls. He was in a hurry. Suddenly, he veered to his left and parked the cart near the patio of the house where the lady was murdered."

Theo, who was holding his breath, said, "Oh my gosh."

Julio looked at him.

"Keep going," Theo said.

"And so this man jumped from the cart, walked to the back door, quickly took off his golf shoes, opened the door, and went inside. The door was not locked and the man was moving fast, like he knew exactly what he was doing. My cousin didn't think much about this because the people who live out there play golf all the time. But it did seem a little odd that the man took off his shoes on the patio. And he did something else that my cousin thought was strange."

"What?"

"The man was wearing a white glove on his left hand. This is normal, no?"

"Yes. Most right-handed golfers wear a glove on the left hand."

"That's what my cousin said. So the man was playing golf somewhere and decided to stop by this house—"

"And he forgot to take off his glove," Theo said.

"Maybe, but here's the strange part. After the man took off his shoes and put them by the door, he reached into his pocket, pulled out another glove, and quickly put it on his right hand. Two white gloves."

The knot in Theo's upper chest now felt like a football.

"Why would the man wear two gloves before he opened the door to the house?" Julio asked.

But Theo didn't answer. His mind was locked on to the image of Mr. Pete Duffy sitting in the courtroom, surrounded by lawyers, with a smug look on his face as if he'd committed the perfect crime and couldn't be caught.

"Which fairway?" Theo asked.

"Number six, on the Creek Course, whatever that means." The Duffy home, Theo said to himself.

"How far away was your cousin?"

"I don't know. I haven't been out there. But he was well hidden. When the man came out of the house, he looked around, very suspiciously, to make sure no one saw him. He had no clue my cousin was watching."

"How long was the man in the house?"

"Not long at all. Again, my cousin was not that suspicious. He finished his lunch and was saying prayers for his family when the man came out of the same door. He walked around the patio for a minute, took his time, looked up and down the fairway, and as he was doing this he removed both gloves and stuffed them in his golf bag. He put his shoes on, then hopped in his golf cart and took off."

"What happened next?"

"At noon, my cousin went back to work. A couple of hours later, he was cutting grass on the North Nine when a friend told him there was some excitement on the Creek Course, said the police were everywhere, that there was a break-in and a woman had been murdered. Throughout the afternoon, the rumors spread like crazy around the golf course, and my cousin soon learned which house it was. He ventured over in one of the utility carts and saw the police hanging around the house. He drove away, in a hurry."

"Did he tell anybody?"

Julio kicked a rock and glanced around again. It was dark now. No one was watching them. "We're still talking secrets, right, Theo?"

"Of course."

"Well, my cousin is illegal. My mother has papers for us, but my cousin has none. The day after the murder, the police arrived with lots of questions. There are two other boys from El Salvador out there, and they're illegal, too. So the boss told my cousin and the other two to get lost, to stay away for a couple of days. That's what they did. Any contact with the police and my cousin would be arrested, put in jail, and then sent back to El Salvador."

"So, he's never told anyone?"

"No. Only me. He was watching television one night and there was a story about the murder. They showed the house, and my cousin recognized it. They showed the man, Mr. Duffy I think, walking down a sidewalk. My cousin said he was pretty sure the man walked just like the man he saw enter the house."

"Why did he tell you?"

"Because I'm his cousin and I'm in school. My English

is good and I have papers. He doesn't understand the court system and he asked me about it. I told him I would try and find out. That's why I'm here, Theo."

"What do you want from me?"

"Tell us what to do. He could be an important witness, right?"

"Oh, yes."

"Then what should my cousin do?"

Run back to El Salvador, Theo thought but didn't say. "Give me a minute," he said, rubbing his jaw. His braces were suddenly aching. He kicked a rock and tried to imagine the storm that would hit if Julio's cousin took the witness stand.

"Is there a reward of some kind?" Julio asked.

"Does he want money?"

"Everybody wants money."

"I don't know, but it might be too late. The trial is half over." Theo kicked another rock and for a moment the two boys studied their feet.

"This is unbelievable," Theo said. He was almost dizzy, and confused. But his thinking was clear enough to know that this was far over his head. The adults would have to deal with it.

There was no way this secret could be kept.

"What?" Julio pressed. He was now staring at Theo, waiting on words of wisdom.

"Where does your cousin live?"

"Near the Quarry. I've never been there."

That's what Theo figured. The Quarry was a rough part of town where lower income people lived. Strattenburg was a safe city, but there was an occasional shooting or a drug bust, and these always seemed to happen around the Quarry.

"Can I talk to your cousin?" Theo asked.

"I don't know, Theo. He's really nervous about this. He's afraid he might get in serious trouble. His job is very important to his family back home."

"I understand. But, I need to nail down the facts before I can decide what to do. How often do you see your cousin?"

"Once or twice a week. He stops by the shelter and checks in with my mother. He's very homesick, and we're the only family he has."

"Does he have a phone?"

"No, but he lives with some other guys and one of them has a phone."

Theo paced around the gravel parking lot, deep in thought. Then he snapped his fingers and said, "Okay, here's the plan. I assume you need help with your algebra homework tonight."

"Uh, I guess."

"Just say yes."

"Yes."

"Good. Get in touch with your cousin and tell him to stop by the shelter in about an hour. I'll run by to help with your homework, and I'll bump into your cousin. Tell him I can be trusted and I will not reveal his secrets to anyone unless he says so. Got it?"

"I'll try. What happens after you talk to him?"

"I don't know. I haven't got that far."

Julio disappeared into the night. Theo returned to his office, where he kept a file on the Duffy case. There were newspaper articles, a copy of the indictment, and Internet searches on Pete Duffy and Clifford Nance, even Jack Hogan, the prosecutor.

All lawyers kept files.

Wednesday night meant Chinese carryout from the Golden Dragon. It was always eaten in the den while the Boones watched Theo's favorite television, reruns of the old *Perry Mason* show.

Mrs. Boone was still with the client, a poor woman who could be heard crying through the locked door. Mr. Boone was on his way to the Golden Dragon when Theo explained that he needed to run by the shelter and spend a few minutes with Julio.

"Don't be too late," Mr. Boone said. "We'll eat at seven."

"I won't." Of course we'll eat at seven.

The firm had a library on the ground floor, near the front. There was a long table in the center of it with leather chairs all around. The walls were covered with shelves loaded with thick books. The important meetings were held in the library. Occasionally groups of lawyers met there for a deposition or a negotiation. Vince the paralegal liked to work there. Theo did, too, when the office wasn't busy. He also enjoyed sneaking into the library late in the afternoon, after the firm had closed, after the others had left.

He and Judge entered and closed the door. He did not turn on the lights. He eased into a leather chair, propped his feet on the table, and stared at the semilit rows of books. Thousands of them. He could barely hear the distant voices of his mother and her client down the hall.

Theo knew of no other kid whose parents worked together as professionals. He knew of no other kid who hung around an office every day after school. Most of his friends were playing baseball or soccer, or swimming, or hanging around the house waiting on dinner. And there he was sitting in a dark law library pondering the events of the past hour.

He loved the place—the rich smell of worn leather and old rugs and dusty law books. The air of importance.

How could it be that he, Theodore Boone, knew the truth about the Duffy murder? Of all the people in Strattenburg, some seventy-five thousand, why him? The town's biggest crime since something bad happened back in the 1950s, and he, Theo, was suddenly in the middle of it.

He had no idea what to do.

CHAPTER 10

There were a few rough-looking men hanging around the entrance of the Highland Street Shelter when Theo parked his bike. He walked through them with a polite "Excuse me" and a metallic smile, and he really had no fear because the men wouldn't bother a kid. The foul odor of stale booze hung in the air.

"Got any change, kid?" a scratchy voice said.

"No, sir," Theo said without slowing down.

Inside, down in the basement, Theo found Julio and his family finishing dinner. His mother spoke passable English, but it was obvious she was surprised to see Theo on a Wednesday night. Theo explained, in what he thought was perfect Spanish, that Julio needed extra help with his algebra. Evidently, she did not understand perfect Spanish because she asked Julio what Theo was talking about. Then Hector began crying about something and she got busy with him.

The cafeteria was packed and overheated, and there were other crying children. Theo and Julio escaped to a small conference room upstairs, one that his mother sometimes used to see her shelter clients.

"Did you talk to your cousin?" Theo asked, after he closed the door.

"Yes. He said he would come, but I don't know. He's very nervous, Theo. Don't be surprised if he doesn't show up."

"Okay. Let's work on the algebra."

"Do we have to?"

"Julio, you're making C's. That's not good enough. You should be making B's."

After ten minutes they were both bored. Theo couldn't concentrate because his mind was on Julio's cousin and the potential bomb his testimony would be. Julio was drifting because he hated algebra. Theo's cell phone rang.

"It's my mom," he said as he flipped it open.

She was leaving the office and was concerned about him.

He assured her that he was fine, working diligently with Julio, and would be home in time for Chinese, even though it might be cold Chinese. What difference did it make, hot or cold?

After he flipped the phone shut, Julio said, "It's pretty cool that you have a cell phone."

"I'm not the only kid in school with a cell phone," Theo said. "And it's only for local calls, no long distance."

"Still cool."

"And it's just a phone, not a computer."

"No one in my class has a cell phone."

"You're just a seventh grader. Wait till next year. Where do you suppose your cousin is right now?"

"Let's call him."

Theo hesitated, then thought, Why not? He didn't have all night to spend with the cousin. He punched the numbers, handed the phone to Julio, who listened for a few seconds and said, "Voice mail."

There was a knock at the door.

The cousin was still wearing a khaki work suit with WAVERLY CREEK GOLF in bold letters across the back of the shirt and in much smaller letters over the front pocket. His matching cap had the same wording. He wasn't much bigger in size than Theo, and certainly looked younger than eighteen or nineteen. His dark eyes danced around wildly, and before he even sat down he gave the clear impression that he was ready to leave.

He refused to shake hands with Theo and refused to give either his first name or his last. In rapid Spanish he went back and forth with Julio. The words were tense.

"He wants to know why he should trust you," Julio said. Theo was thankful for the interpretation because he'd understood almost none of the Spanish.

He said, "Look, Julio, how about a quick review? He came to you, you came to me, and now I'm here. I didn't start this process. If he wants to leave, then good-bye. I'll be happy to go home." It was tough talk and it sounded pretty strong in English. Julio passed it along in Spanish, and the cousin glared at Theo as if he'd been insulted.

Theo did not want to leave. He knew he should. He knew better than to get involved. He'd been telling himself to butt out, but the truth was that Theo relished being exactly where he was at that moment. "Tell him he can trust me and that I will not tell anyone what he says," he said to Julio.

Julio passed it along, and the cousin seemed to relax a little.

It was obvious to Theo that the cousin was deeply troubled and wanted some help. Julio kept rattling on in Spanish. He was heaping praise upon Theo, who understood some of it.

The cousin smiled.

Theo had printed a color Google Earth Search map of the Creek Course, and he had marked the Duffy home. The cousin, still unnamed, began to tell his story. He pointed to a spot in some trees in a dogleg on the sixth fairway, and spoke rapidly about what he had seen. He'd been sitting on some timbers near a streambed, just inside the tree line, eating his lunch, minding his own business, when he saw the man enter the house from the rear door and exit a few minutes later. Julio gamely hung on with his interpretation, often stopping his cousin so he could do the English for Theo. Theo, to his credit, began to understand more and more of the Spanish as he grew accustomed to the cousin's speech patterns.

The cousin described the frenzy around the golf course after the police showed up and the gossip spread. According to one of his friends, a kid from Honduras who waited tables in the clubhouse grill, Mr. Duffy was having a late lunch and a drink when he got the news that his wife had been found. He made a scene, hustled out, jumped in his golf cart, and raced home. This friend said that Mr. Duffy was wearing a black sweater, tan slacks, and a maroon golf cap. It was a perfect match, said the cousin. The same outfit worn by the man he saw enter the Duffy home and exit just minutes later.

From his file, Theo produced four photographs of Pete Duffy. All four had been found online, in the archives of the Strattenburg daily newspaper. He had enlarged them to 8 by 10 inches. He spread them on the table and waited. The cousin could not identify Mr. Duffy. He estimated that he was between sixty to a hundred yards away when he was having his quiet lunch and saw the man. The man he'd seen looked very similar to the one in the photographs, but the cousin could not be certain. He was certain, though, of what the man was wearing.

A positive identification by the cousin would be helpful, but not crucial. It would be easy to establish how Mr. Duffy was dressed, and the fact that a witness saw a man in the identical clothing enter the home just minutes before the murder would nail a conviction, at least in Theo's opinion.

As Theo listened to Julio translate into Spanish, he watched the cousin closely. There was no doubt he was telling the truth. Why would he not tell the truth? He had nothing to gain by lying, and plenty to lose! His story was believable. And, it fit perfectly into the prosecution's theory of guilt. The problem, though, was that the prosecution had no idea such a witness even existed.

Theo listened, and again asked himself what he should do next.

The cousin was talking even faster, as if the dam had finally broken and he wanted to unload everything. Julio was working even harder to translate. Theo typed feverishly on his laptop, taking as many notes as possible. He stopped the narrative, asked Julio to repeat something, then off they went again.

When Theo could think of no more questions, he glanced at his watch and was surprised at how late it was. It was after 7:00 p.m. and his parents would not be happy that he was late for dinner. He said he needed to leave. The cousin asked what would happen next.

"I'm not sure," Theo answered. "Give me some time. Let me sleep on it."

"But you promised not to tell," Julio said.

"I won't tell, Julio. Not until we—the three of us—decide on a plan."

"If he gets scared, he'll just disappear," Julio said, nodding at his cousin. "He cannot get caught. Understand?"

"Of course I understand."

———

The chicken chow mein was colder than usual, but Theo had little appetite for it. The Boones ate on TV trays in the den. Judge, who had refused dog food since the first week as a member of the family, ate from his bowl near the television. There was nothing wrong with his appetite.

"Why aren't you eating?" his mother said, her chopsticks in midair.

"I am eating."

"You seem preoccupied," his father said. He used a fork.

"Yes, you do," his mother agreed. "Something happen at the shelter?"

"No, just thinking about Julio and his family and how difficult it must be for them."

"You're such a sweet kid, Teddy."

If you only knew, Theo thought.

Perry Mason, in black and white, was in the midst of a big trial, and he was on the verge of losing the case. The judge was fed up with him. The jurors looked skeptical. The prosecutor was full of confidence. Suddenly, Perry looked into the crowd of spectators and called the name of a surprise witness. The witness took the stand and began telling a story far different from the one the prosecutor had put forth. The new story made perfect sense. The surprise witness withstood the cross-examination, and the jury found in favor of Perry Mason's client.

Another happy ending. Another courtroom victory.

"Doesn't work that way," Mrs. Boone said. It was something she managed to say at least three times during every episode. "No such thing as a surprise witness."

Theo saw an opening. "But what if a witness suddenly appeared? One that was crucial to finding the truth? And one that no one knew about?"

"If no one knew about him, how would he find his way to the courtroom?" Mr. Boone asked.

"What if he just appeared?" Theo replied. "What if an eyewitness read about the trial in the newspaper, or saw something about it on television, and came forward. No one knew he existed. No one knew he witnessed the crime. What would the judge do?"

It was rare that Theo could stump, even briefly, the other two lawyers in the family. His parents thought about his question. A couple of things were certain at this point. One, both parents would have an opinion. Two, there was no way they would agree.

His mother went first. "The prosecution cannot use a witness it has not disclosed to the court and the defense. The rules prohibit surprise witnesses."

"But," his father said, almost interrupting and obviously ready to argue, "if the prosecution doesn't know about a witness, then the prosecution cannot disclose his identity. A trial is all about finding the truth. Denying an eyewitness the chance to testify is the same as hiding the truth."

"The rules are the rules."

"But the rules can be modified by the judge when necessary."

"A conviction would not stand up on appeal."

"I'm not so sure about that."

Back and forth, back and forth. Theo grew quiet. He thought of reminding his parents that neither specialized in criminal law, but such a comment would probably draw fire from both. Such discussions were common in the Boone household, and Theo had learned much about the law over dinner, on the front porch, even riding down the road in the backseat.

For example, he had learned that his parents, as lawyers, were considered to be officers of the court. And as such, they had a duty to aid in the administration of justice. If other lawyers violated ethics, or if the police broke the rules, or if a judge got out of line, then his parents were supposed to take appropriate action. Many lawyers ignored this responsibility, according to his parents, but not them.

Theo was afraid to tell them about Julio's cousin. Their

sense of duty would probably force them to go straight to Judge Gantry. The cousin would be picked up by the police, dragged into court, forced to testify, then detained as an illegal immigrant. They would put him in jail, then some sort of detention center, where, according to Mr. Mount, he might spend months waiting to get shipped back to El Salvador.

Theo's credibility would be ruined. A family would be seriously harmed.

But, a guilty man would be convicted. Otherwise, Pete Duffy would probably walk out of court a free man. He would get away with murder.

Theo choked down another bite of cold chicken.

He knew he would sleep little.

CHAPTER
11

The nightmares stopped just before sunrise, and Theo abandoned the notion of somehow finding meaningful rest. He stared at the ceiling of his bedroom for a long time, waiting for sounds that his parents were up and moving about. He said good morning to Judge, who slept under the bed.

Theo had convinced himself many times throughout the night that he had no choice but to sit down with them early that morning and tell them the story of Julio's cousin. He'd changed his mind many times. And he could not, he decided as he finally eased out of his bed, force himself to violate the promise he'd made to Julio and his cousin. He could not tell anyone. If a guilty man was about to walk free, then it wasn't Theo's problem.

Or was it?

He made the usual noise as he went about his morning ritual—shower, teeth, braces, the daily torture of deciding what to wear. As always, he thought of Elsa and her irritating habit of quickly inspecting his shirt, pants, and shoes to make sure it all matched and that none of it had been worn in the past three days.

He heard his father leave a few minutes before seven. He heard his mother in the den watching an early morning television show. At exactly seven thirty, Theo closed the door to his bathroom, opened his cell phone, and called Uncle Ike.

Ike was not an early riser. His sad little career of a small-time tax man wasn't very demanding, and he didn't start the day with a rush of enthusiasm. His work was dreary, something he had mentioned to Theo on many occasions. And there was another problem. Ike drank too much, and this unfortunate habit made for slow mornings. Over the years, Theo had heard the adults whispering about Ike's drinking. Elsa had once asked Vince a question dealing with Ike, and Vince replied with a curt, "Maybe if he's sober." Theo wasn't supposed to hear that, but Theo heard a lot more around the office than the others knew.

The call was finally answered with a scratchy and rude, "Is this Theo?"

"Yes, Ike, good morning. Sorry to bother you so early." Theo was speaking as softly as possible into the phone.

"No problem, Theo. I assume you have something on your mind."

"Yes, can we talk this morning, early? At your office? Something real important has come up and I'm not sure I can discuss it with my parents."

"Well, sure, Theo. What time?"

"Maybe a few minutes after eight. School starts at eight thirty. If I leave too early Mom will get suspicious."

"Sure. I'd love to."

"Thanks, Ike."

Theo hurried through breakfast, kissed his mom good-bye, spoke to Judge, and was on his bike racing down Mallard Lane at straight-up eight o'clock.

Ike was at his desk with a tall paper cup of steaming coffee and a huge cinnamon swirl coated with at least an inch of frosting. It looked delicious, but Theo had just finished his cereal. Plus, he had no appetite.

"Are you okay?" Ike said as Theo sat down, on the very edge of his chair.

"I guess. I need to talk to someone in confidence, someone I can trust, someone who knows something about the law."

"Have you murdered someone? Robbed a bank?"

"No."

"You seem awfully uptight," Ike said as he pulled off a huge bite of the cinnamon swirl and stuffed it in his mouth.

"It's the Duffy case, Ike. I might know something about whether Mr. Duffy is guilty or not."

Ike kept chewing as he leaned forward on his elbows. The wrinkles around his eyes squeezed together as he glared at Theo. "Go on."

"There is a witness out there, a guy nobody knows about, who saw something at the time of the murder."

"And you know who it is?"

"Yes, and I promised not to tell."

"How in the world did you come across this guy?"

"Through a kid at school. I can't tell you anything else, Ike. I promised I wouldn't."

Ike swallowed hard, then grabbed the cup and took a long sip of the coffee. His eyes never left Theo. He really wasn't that surprised. His nephew knew more lawyers, court clerks, judges, and policemen than anyone else in town.

"And whatever this unknown witness saw out there would have a big impact on the trial, is that right?" Ike asked.

"Yes."

"Has this witness talked to the police or lawyers or anyone involved with the case?"

"No."

"And this witness is unwilling to come forward at this time?"

"Yes."

"This witness is afraid of something?"

"Yes."

"Would the testimony of this witness help convict Mr. Duffy, or would it help acquit him?"

"Convict, no doubt."

"Have you talked to this witness?"

"Yes."

"And you believe him?"

"Yes. He's telling the truth."

Another long drink of coffee. A smacking of the lips. Ike's eyes were drilling holes in Theo's.

Ike continued. "Today is Thursday, the third full day of trial. From what I hear, Judge Gantry is determined to finish this week, even if that means holding court on Saturday. So the trial is probably half finished."

Theo nodded. His uncle stuffed another large bite into his mouth and chewed slowly. A minute passed.

Ike finally swallowed and said, "So the question is, obviously, what, if anything, could or should be done about this witness at this point in the trial?"

"That's it," Theo said.

"Yes, and from what I gather Mr. Jack Hogan needs a few surprises. The prosecution started with a weak case and it's only grown weaker."

"I thought you weren't following the trial."

"I have friends, Theo. Sources."

Ike jumped to his feet and walked to the far end of the room where some old shelves were filled with law books. He ran a finger along the spines of several, then snatched one off a shelf and began thumbing through the pages. He returned to his desk, sat down, placed the book in front of him, and searched for whatever was on his mind. Finally, after a long silence, he said, "Here it is. Under our rules of procedure, a judge in a criminal trial has the authority to declare a mistrial if the judge thinks that something improper has occurred. It gives a few examples: a juror gets contacted by someone with an interest in the outcome; an important witness gets sick or can't testify for some reason; key evidence disappears. Stuff like that."

Theo knew this. "Does it cover surprise witnesses?" he asked.

"Not specifically, but it's a pretty broad rule that allows the judge to do whatever he thinks is right. The argument could be made that the absence of an important witness is grounds for a mistrial."

"What happens after a mistrial?"

"The charges are not dismissed. Another trial is rescheduled."

"When?"

"It's up to the judge, but in this case I suspect Gantry wouldn't wait too long. A couple of months. Enough time for this secret witness to get his act together."

Theo's mind was racing so fast he couldn't decide what to say next.

Ike said, "So, Theo, the question is, How do you convince Judge Gantry to declare a mistrial before the case goes to the jury? Before the jury finds Mr. Duffy not guilty, when in fact he is guilty?"

"I don't know. That's where you come in, Ike. I need your help."

Ike shoved the book aside and peeled off another piece of the cinnamon swirl. He chewed it while he pondered the situation. "Here's what we do," he said, still chewing. "You go to school. I'll go over to the courtroom and have a look. I'll do some more research, maybe talk to a friend or two. I won't use your name. Believe me, Theo, I'll always protect you. Can you call me during lunch?"

"Sure."

"Take off."

When Theo was at the door, Ike said, "Why haven't you told your parents?"

"You think I should?"

"Not yet. Maybe later."

"They're very ethical, Ike. You know that. They are officers of the court and they might force me to reveal what I know. It's complicated."

"Theo, it's too complicated for a thirteen-year-old."

"I think I agree."

"Call me during lunch."

"Will do, Ike. Thanks."

During recess, as Theo was hustling away to find April, someone called his name from down the hall. It was Sandy Coe, racing to catch up.

"Theo," he said. "Got a minute?"

"Uh, sure."

"Look, I just wanted to tell you that my parents went to see that bankruptcy lawyer, that Mozingo guy, and he promised them that we are not going to lose our house."

"That's great, Sandy."

"He said they would have to go through a bankruptcy—all that stuff you explained to me—but in the end we get to keep the house." Sandy reached into his backpack, pulled out a small envelope, and handed it to Theo. "This is from my mom. I told her about you, and I think this is a thank-you note."

Theo reluctantly took it. "She didn't have to, Sandy. It was nothing."

"Nothing? Theo, we get to keep our house."

And with that, Theo noticed the moisture in Sandy's eyes. He was ready to cry. Theo fist-bumped him and said, "My pleasure, Sandy. And if I can help again, just let me know."

"Thanks, Theo."

During Government, Mr. Mount asked Theo to give the class an update on the Duffy trial. Theo explained that the prosecution was attempting to prove that Mr. and Mrs. Duffy had been through a rocky marriage and that they had almost filed for divorce two years earlier. Several of their friends had been called to testify, but they had been embarrassed—in Theo's opinion—by harsh cross-examinations from Mr. Clifford Nance.

For a second, Theo thought about opening his laptop and reading the courtroom dialogue hot off the press, but then thought better of it. He wasn't committing a crime by hacking into the court reporter's site, but there was definitely something wrong with it.

As soon as class was over and the boys headed for the cafeteria, Theo ducked into a restroom and called Ike. It was almost twelve thirty. "He's gonna walk," Ike said as he answered the phone. "No way Hogan can get a conviction."

"How much did you watch?" Theo asked, hiding in a stall.

"All morning. Clifford Nance is too good and Hogan has lost his way. I watched the jurors. They don't like Pete Duffy, but the proof isn't there. He'll walk."

"But he's guilty, Ike."

"If you say so, Theo. But I don't know what you know. No one does."

"What do we do?"

"I'm still working on it. Stop by after school."

"You got it."

CHAPTER
12

The most popular girl in the eighth grade was a curly-haired brunette named Hallie. She was very cute and outgoing and loved to flirt. She was the captain of the cheerleaders, but she could also play. None of the boys would challenge her in tennis and she had once beaten Brian in both the 100-meter freestyle and 50-meter breaststroke. Since her interests centered around athletics, Theo was on her B list. Maybe even C.

But because her dog had a temper, Theo was about to move up.

The dog was a schnauzer that frequently became irritated when left alone at home throughout the day. Somehow the dog escaped through a pet door, dug under a fence around the backyard, and was picked up by Animal Control half a mile from home. Theo heard this story as he was finishing lunch. Hallie and two of her friends rushed to the table where Theo was eating, and the story spilled forth. Hallie was distraught, in tears, and Theo couldn't help but notice how cute she was even when she was crying. It was a big moment for Theo.

"Has this happened before?" he asked.

She wiped her cheeks and said, "Yes. Rocky was picked up a few months ago."

"Will they gas him?" Edward asked. Edward was part of the group that had gathered around Theo and Hallie and her friends. Hallie usually attracted a crowd of boys. The thought of her dog getting gassed made her cry even more.

"Shut up," Theo snapped at Edward, who was a klutz anyway. "No, they won't gas him."

Hallie said, "My dad is out of town and my mother is seeing patients until late this afternoon. I don't know what to do."

Theo was shoving his lunch aside and opening his laptop. "Take it easy, Hallie. I've done this before." He punched a few keys while the group inched closer together. "I assume the dog is licensed," Theo said.

Strattenburg had an ordinance that required every dog

to be licensed and accounted for. Strays were picked up and kept at the Pound for thirty days. If no one adopted a stray after thirty days, then the poor dog was put to sleep. Or "gassed," as Edward so crudely put it. But they didn't really use gas.

Hallie's family was more affluent than most. Her father ran a company and her mother was a busy doctor. Of course their dog would be properly licensed. "Yes," she said. "In my dad's name."

"And that is?" Theo asked, tapping keys.

"Walter Kershaw."

Theo typed. Everyone waited. The crying had stopped.

"Okay," Theo said as he pecked away and studied the screen. "I'm just checking the Animal Control Intake Log." More pecking. "And here it is. Rocky was taken into the Pound at nine thirty this morning. He's charged with violating the leash law, his second offense this year. The fine will be twenty bucks, plus eight more for boarding. A third offense will get him ten days in the slammer and a fine of a hundred bucks."

"When can I get him?" Hallie asked.

"Animal Court is held from four until six each afternoon, four days a week, closed on Monday. Can you be in court this afternoon?"

"I guess, but don't I need my parents?"

"Nope. I'll be there. I've done it before."

"Doesn't she need a real lawyer?" Edward asked.

"No, not in Animal Court. Even a moron like you could get through it."

"What about the money?" Hallie asked.

"I can't charge. I don't have my license yet."

"Not you, Theo. The money for the fine?"

"Oh, that. Here's the plan. I'll file a Notice of Retrieval, online. This means that Rocky is basically pleading guilty to a leash law violation, which is just a minor offense, and that you, as one of the owners, will pay a fine and retrieve him from the Pound. After school, you run by the hospital, see your mother, get the money, and I'll meet you at the courthouse at four o'clock."

"Thanks, Theo. Will Rocky be there?"

"No. Rocky stays at the Pound. You and your mother can pick him up later."

"Why can't I get him in court?" she asked.

Theo was often amazed at the ridiculous questions his friends asked. Animal Court was the lowest of all courts. Its nickname was Kitty Court, and it was treated like an unwanted stepchild by the judicial system. The judge was a lawyer who'd been kicked out of every firm in town. He wore blue jeans and combat boots and was humiliated to have such a low position. The rules allowed any person with an animal in trouble to appear without a lawyer and handle their own case. Most lawyers avoided Kitty Court because it was so far beneath their dignity. Its hearing room was in the basement of the courthouse, far away from the big leagues.

Did Hallie really believe that the officers hauled over a bunch of dogs and cats, chained and muzzled, every afternoon to get processed and returned to their owners? Criminal defendants were brought from jail and kept in the holding pen where they waited for their turn in front of a judge. But not dogs and cats.

A sarcastic reply almost escaped Theo's lips, but instead he smiled at Hallie, even cuter now, and said, "Sorry, Hallie, but it doesn't work that way. You'll have Rocky at home tonight, safe and sound."

"Thanks, Theo. You're the best."

On a normal day, those words would have rattled around Theo's ears for hours, but this was not a normal day. He was too preoccupied with the trial of Pete Duffy. Ike was in the courtroom, and Theo texted him throughout the afternoon.

Theo wrote: > U there? Update plse.

Ike responded: >> Yep balcony. Big crowd. State rested 2 pm.

Nice job raising doubt w divorce talk and old golfin buddies.

> Enough proof?

>> No way. This guys walkin. Unless . . .

> U got a plan?

>> Still workin on it. U comin to court?

> Maybe. Whats hapnin?

>> First witness for defense. Biz partner of Duffy. Boring.

> Gotta run. Chemistry. Later.

>> I want an A in Chemistry. OK?

> No problem.

Though Animal Court got little respect among the lawyers of Strattenburg, it was seldom dull. The case involved a boa constrictor named Herman, and evidently Herman had a knack for escaping. His adventures would not have been a problem if his owner lived out in the country, in a more rural setting. However, the owner, a punkish-looking thirty-year-old with tattoos crawling up his neck, lived in a crowded apartment building in a lesser part of town. A neighbor had been horrified to find Herman stretched across his kitchen floor early one morning as he was about to fix a bowl of oatmeal.

The neighbor was furious. Herman's owner was indignant. Things were tense. Theo and Hallie sat in folding chairs, the only spectators in the tiny courtroom. The library at Boone & Boone was bigger and far nicer.

Herman was on display. He was in a large wire cage, perched on a corner of the bench, not far from Judge Yeck, who eyed him carefully. The only other official in court was an elderly clerk who'd been there for years and was known to be the grouchiest old bag in the entire building. She wanted no part of Herman. She had retreated to a far corner and still looked frightened.

"How would you like it, Judge?" the neighbor said. "Living in the same building with that creature, never knowing if it might come slithering across your bed while you're asleep."

"He's harmless," the owner said. "He doesn't bite."

"Harmless? What about a heart attack? It's not right, Judge. You gotta protect us."

"He doesn't look harmless," Judge Yeck said, and everyone looked at Herman, who was tangled around a fake tree limb, inside the cage, motionless, apparently asleep, unimpressed by the gravity of the proceedings.

"Isn't he rather large for a red-tailed boa?" Judge Yeck asked, as if he'd seen his share of boa constrictors.

"Eighty-six inches, as best I can tell," the owner said proudly. "A little on the long side."

"You have other snakes in your apartment?" the judge asked.

"Several."

"How many?"

"Four."

"Oh my God," the neighbor said. He looked faint.

"All boas?" the judge asked.

"Three boas and a king snake."

"May I ask why?"

The owner shifted his weight, shrugged, said, "Some people like parrots, others like gerbils. Dogs, cats, horses, goats. Me, I like snakes. They're nice pets."

"Nice pets," the neighbor hissed.

"Is this the first time one has escaped?" Judge Yeck asked.

"Yes," said the owner.

"No," said the neighbor.

"Well, that clears things up."

As fascinating as it was, Theo was having trouble focusing on Herman and his problems. Two things diverted his attention. The most obvious was the fact that Hallie was sitting very close, and this made the moment one of Theo's finest. But even this was overshadowed by the more serious issue of what to do about Julio's cousin.

The murder trial was zipping right along. The lawyers and witnesses would soon be finished. Judge Gantry would soon give the case to the jury. The clock was ticking.

"You gotta protect us, Judge," the neighbor said again.

"What do you want me to do?" Judge Yeck shot back. His patience was running out.

"Can't you order it destroyed?"

"You want the death penalty for Herman?"

"Why not? There are children in our building."

"Seems kind of harsh," Judge Yeck said. It was obvious he was not going to order the death of Herman.

"Come on," the owner said in disgust. "He's never harmed anyone."

"Can you make sure the snakes stay in your apartment?" the judge asked.

"Yes. You have my word."

"Here's what we're going to do," Judge Yeck said. "Take Herman home. I never want to see him again. We don't have a place to keep him at the Pound. We don't want him at the Pound. No one at the Pound likes Herman. Do you understand this?"

"I guess," the owner said.

"If Herman escapes again, or if your snakes are caught outside of your apartment, then I have no choice but to order them destroyed. All of them. Clear enough?"

"Yes, Your Honor. I promise."

"I bought an ax," the neighbor said hotly. "A long-handle ax. Cost me twelve bucks at Home Depot." He pointed angrily at Herman. "I see that snake, or any snake, in my apartment, or anywhere else, you won't have to get involved, Your Honor, sir."

"Settle down."

"I swear I'll kill him. Should've killed him this time, but I wasn't thinking. And, I didn't have an ax."

"That's enough," Judge Yeck said. "Case dismissed."

The owner rushed forward, grabbed the heavy cage, and gently lifted it off the bench. Herman wasn't fazed. He showed little interest in the debate over his death. The neighbor stomped out of the courtroom. The owner and Herman loitered about, then left, too.

After the doors were slammed, the clerk eased back to her seat near the bench. The judge looked at some paperwork, then glanced up at Theo and Hallie. There was no one else in the courtroom.

"Well, hello, Mr. Boone," he said.

"Good afternoon, Judge," Theo said.

"You have business before the court?"

"Yes, sir. I need to retrieve a dog."

The judge picked up a sheet of paper, his docket. "Rocky?" he asked.

"Yes, sir."

"Very well. You may come forward."

Theo and Hallie walked through the small swinging gate to the only table. Theo showed her where to sit. He remained standing, just like a real lawyer.

"Proceed," Judge Yeck said, obviously enjoying the moment and realizing that young Theo Boone was working hard to impress his very cute client. The judge smiled as he remembered Theo's first appearance in his courtroom. He had been one frightened boy as he frantically worked to rescue a runaway mutt, one that he took home and named Judge.

"Well, Your Honor," Theo began properly. "Rocky is a miniature schnauzer registered to Mr. Walter Kershaw, who is out of town on business. His wife, Dr. Phyllis Kershaw, is a pediatrician and could not be here. My client is their daughter, Hallie, who is in the eighth grade with me at the middle school." Theo sort of waved at Hallie, who was terrified but also confident that Theo knew what he was doing.

Judge Yeck smiled down at Hallie. Then he said, "I see this is the second offense."

"Yes, sir," Theo said. "The first offense was four months ago and Mr. Kershaw handled matters at the Pound."

"And Rocky is in custody?"

"Yes, sir."

"You can't deny the fact that he was loose, can you?"

"No, sir, but I ask the court to waive both the fine and the boarding fee."

"On what grounds?"

"Sir, the owners took all reasonable steps to prevent their dog from getting out. As always, Rocky was left in a secure place. The house was locked. The alarm was on. The gates to the backyard fencing were closed. They did everything possible to prevent this. Rocky has quite a temper and often becomes irritated when he's left alone. He likes to run away when he gets out. The owners know this. They were not being careless."

The judge removed his reading glasses and chewed on a stem as he pondered this. "Is this true, Hallie?" he asked.

"Oh, yes, sir. We're very concerned about Rocky getting out."

"This is a very clever dog, Your Honor," Theo said. "He somehow broke through a pet door in the laundry and escaped to the backyard, where he dug a hole under the fence."

"Suppose he does it again."

"The owners intend to beef up security, sir."

"Very well. I'll waive the fine and fee. But if Rocky gets caught again, I'll double all fines and fees. Understand?"

"Yes, Your Honor."

"Case dismissed."

As they were walking down the hallway on the first floor, headed for the main entrance, Hallie slid her hand around Theo's left elbow. Arm in arm. He instinctively slowed down a little. What a moment. "You're a great lawyer, Theo," she said.

"Not really. Not yet."

"Why don't you call me sometime?" she asked.

Why? Now that was a good question. Probably because he assumed she was too busy talking to all the other boys. She changed boyfriends every other month. He'd never even thought of calling her.

"I'll do that," he said. But he knew he wouldn't. He wasn't exactly looking for a girlfriend, and besides, April would be devastated if he began chasing a flirt like Hallie.

Girls, murder trials, secret witnesses. Life was suddenly very complicated.

CHAPTER
13

After a long good-bye, Theo came back to Earth. He practically ran up the stairs to the second floor, then to the balcony, where he found Ike in the front row. He slid in beside him. It was almost 5:00 p.m.

The witness was the insurance agent who'd sold the $1 million policy to the Duffys just over two years earlier. Clifford Nance was slowly walking the agent through his dealings with the couple. He carefully made the point that two policies were purchased, one insuring the life of Mrs. Myra Duffy, and the other for Mr. Peter Duffy. Both were for $1 million. Both policies replaced existing policies that would pay $500,000 in the event of either death. There was nothing unusual about the transaction. The agent testified that it was rather typical—a married couple wisely increasing their coverage to protect each other in the event of an untimely death. Both Duffys knew exactly what they were doing and did not hesitate to upgrade their policies.

By the time Clifford Nance finished with the direct examination, the $1 million payoff sounded far less suspicious. Jack Hogan threw a few punches on cross-examination but nothing landed. When the agent was finished, Judge Gantry decided to call it a day.

Theo watched the jury file out of the courtroom as everyone waited, then he watched the defense team huddle around Pete Duffy and offer smug smiles and a few handshakes for another productive day in court. They were very confident. Omar Cheepe was not present.

"I don't want to talk around here," Ike said in a low voice. "Can you run by the office?"

"Sure."

"Now?"

"I'm right behind you."

Ten minutes later they were in Ike's office with the door locked. Ike opened a small refrigerator on the floor behind his desk. "I have Budweiser and Sprite."

"Budweiser," Theo said.

Ike gave him a Sprite and popped the top of a can of Bud for himself. "Your options are limited," he said, then took a sip.

"I figured."

"First, you can do nothing. Tomorrow is Friday, and it looks like the defense will rest by midafternoon. Rumor is that Pete Duffy will testify, and go last. The jury might even get the case by late afternoon. If you do nothing, then the jury retires to the jury room and considers its verdict. They can find him guilty, or not guilty, or they can split and not be able to reach a verdict. A hung jury."

Theo knew all this. In the past five years he'd watched far more trials than Ike.

His uncle continued: "Second, you can go to this mysterious witness and try to convince him to come forward immediately. I'm not sure what Judge Gantry would do now if confronted with this kind of testimony. I'm sure he's never been in this position, but he's a good judge and he'll do what's right."

"This guy is not about to come forward. He's too scared."

"Okay, that leads to your third option. You can go to the judge anyway, and without revealing the name of the witness—"

"I don't know his name."

"But you know who he is, right?"

"Right."

"Do you know where he lives?"

"The general area. I don't know his address."

"Do you know where he works?"

"Maybe."

Ike stared at him as he took another sip from the can. He swiped his lips with the back of a hand. "As I was saying, without revealing his identity, explain to the judge that a crucial witness is missing from this trial and his absence will likely lead to the wrong verdict. The judge, of course, will want details: Who is he? Where does he work? How did he become a witness? What, exactly, did he see? And so on. I suspect Judge Gantry will have a thousand questions and if you don't answer them, then he might get upset."

"I don't like any of the three options," Theo said.

"Nor do I."

"Then what should I do, Ike?"

"Leave it alone, Theo. Don't stick your nose into this mess. It's no place for a kid. It's no place for an adult. The jury is about to make the wrong decision, but based on the evidence, you can't blame them. The system doesn't always work, you know. Look at all the innocent people who've been sent to death row. Look at the guilty people who get off. Mistakes happen, Theo. Leave it alone."

"But this mistake hasn't happened yet, and it can be prevented."

"I'm not sure it can be prevented. It's highly unlikely that Judge Gantry will stop a big trial that's almost over just because he hears about a potential witness. That's a stretch, Theo."

It did seem unlikely, and Theo had to agree. "I guess you're right."

"Of course I'm right, Theo. You're just a kid. Butt out."

"Okay, Ike."

There was a long pause as they stared at each other, waiting for the other to speak. Finally, Ike said, "Promise me you won't do something stupid."

"Like what?"

"Like to go the judge. I know you two are buddies."

Another pause.

"Promise me, Theo."

"I promise I won't do anything before I talk with you."

"Fair enough."

Theo jumped to his feet. "I need to go. I have a lot of homework."

"How's Spanish?"

"Great."

"I hear that teacher is really something. Madame, what's her name?"

"Madame Monique. She's very good. How do you know—"

"I keep up, Theo. I'm not some crazy recluse like everybody thinks. Are they offering Chinese yet in this school system?"

"Maybe in the upper school."

"I think you should start Chinese, on your own. It's the language of the future, Theo."

Once again, he was irked that his uncle was so free to give advice that was not asked for and certainly not needed. "I'll think about it, Ike. Right now I'm pretty loaded."

"I might watch the trial tomorrow," Ike said. "I kind of enjoyed it today. Text me."

"You got it, Ike."

Boone & Boone was quiet when Theo made his appearance a few minutes after 6:00 p.m. Elsa, Vince, and Dorothy were long gone. Mrs. Boone was at home, no doubt skimming the pages of another bad novel. Her book club would meet at seven, at the home of Mrs. Esther Guthridge, for dinner and wine and a discussion of almost everything except their book of the month. The club had ten women in all, and they took turns selecting the books. Theo could not remember the last one that his mother enjoyed, not even the ones she'd picked. Each month she could be heard complaining about whatever book she was supposed to be reading. It seemed an odd way to run a club, at least in Theo's opinion.

Woods Boone was stuffing his briefcase when Theo entered the upstairs office. Theo often wondered why his father crammed files and books into his briefcase and hauled it home every night as if he just might work until midnight. He did not. He never worked at home, never touched the briefcase, which he always placed under a table in the foyer near the front door. And there it sat, all night, until Mr. Boone left early in the morning for breakfast and then to the office, where he unpacked the briefcase and flung its contents onto his terribly disorganized desk. Theo suspected that the stuffing was always the same—same books, files, papers.

He had noticed that lawyers seldom go anywhere without a briefcase. Maybe to lunch. His mother hauled hers home, too, but she occasionally unlatched it and read some of its contents.

"A good day at school?" Mr. Boone asked.

"Great."

"That's good. Listen, Theo, your mother has book club tonight. I'm going over to Judge Plankmore's for a little while. The old guy is fading fast and I need to sit with him for a couple of hours. Won't be long before there's a funeral."

"Sure, Dad. No problem."

Judge Plankmore was at least ninety years old and dying from multiple causes. He was a legend in the Strattenburg legal world and most of the lawyers adored him.

"There's some leftover spaghetti you can zap in the microwave."

"I'll be fine, Dad. Don't worry. I'll probably study here for an hour or so, then go home. I'll take care of Judge."

"You're sure?"

"No problem."

Theo went to his office, unloaded his backpack, and was trying to concentrate on his Chemistry homework when there was a slight knock on the back door. It was Julio, for the second day in a row.

"Can we talk outside?" he said, very nervous.

"Come on in," Theo said. "Everyone's gone. We can talk in here."

"Are you sure?"

"Yes. What's up?"

Julio sat down. Theo closed the door.

"I talked with my cousin an hour ago. He's very nervous. There were policemen at the golf course today. He thinks you've told them about him."

"Come on, Julio. I haven't told anyone. I swear it."

"Then why were the police out there?"

"I have no idea. Did they want to talk to your cousin?"

"I don't think so. He disappeared when he saw the police car."

"Were the policemen wearing uniforms?"

"I think so."

"Were they driving a car that was obviously a police car?"

"I think so."

"Look, Julio, I gave you my word. I haven't told the police. And if they wanted to talk to your cousin about the murder, they wouldn't be wearing uniforms and they wouldn't be driving a car with the word POLICE painted on the doors. No way. They would be detectives, with coats and ties and unmarked cars."

"Are you sure?"

"Yes, I'm sure."

"Okay."

"I guess your cousin gets pretty nervous when he sees policemen, right?"

"Most illegals do."

"That's my point. Tell your cousin to relax."

"Relax? It's hard to relax when you might get arrested any day of your life."

"Good point."

Julio was still nervous, his eyes darting around the small room as if someone else might be listening. There was a long, awkward pause while each waited for the other to say something. Finally, Julio said, "There's something else."

"What?"

His hands were shaking as he unbuttoned his shirt and pulled out a clear plastic bag, a Ziploc. He laid it carefully on Theo's desk as if it were a gift he never wanted to touch again. In it were two objects, white in color, slightly worn, and wadded.

Golf gloves.

"My cousin gave me this," he said. "Two golf gloves, worn by the man he saw go into the house where the lady was killed. One for the right hand, one for the left. The right hand is new. The left hand has been used."

Theo gawked at the gloves in the bag, but couldn't move

and for a moment couldn't speak. "Where did he find—"

"When the man came out of the house, he took the gloves off and put them in his golf bag. Later, on the fourteenth tee, he placed these gloves in the trash bucket next to the water cooler. My cousin's job is to empty the trash twice a day. He saw the man and thought it was strange that he was throwing away good gloves."

"Did the man see him?"

"I don't think so. If he had, I don't think he would have left the gloves behind."

"And this is the man who's on trial now for the murder?"

"Yes, I believe so. My cousin is pretty sure. He saw him on television."

"Why did he keep the gloves?"

"The boys out there go through the trash, looking for stuff. My cousin took the gloves, and within a couple of days he was suspicious. I guess there's a lot of gossip around a golf course and there was talk about the dead woman. So my cousin hid the gloves. Now he's scared and he thinks the police are watching him. If they find him with the gloves, who knows? He's afraid he might get in trouble."

"The police are not watching him."

"I will tell him this."

A long pause, then Theo nodded at the gloves, still afraid to touch anything. "And what do we do with these?"

"I'm not keeping them."

"That's what I was afraid of."

"You know what to do, right, Theo?"

"I have no clue. Right now I'm wondering how I got in the middle of this mess."

"Can't you just drop them off at the police station?"

Theo bit his tongue, preventing a phrase or two that would certainly be taken as sarcastic or cruel or both. How could Julio be expected to understand the system? Sure, Julio, I'll just run by the police station, give the receptionist a Ziploc with two golf gloves, explain that they were worn by the nice man who's now on trial for killing his wife, and who in fact did kill his wife because I, Theo Boone, know the truth because I, for some reason, have talked to a key witness no one else knows about it, and, please, Miss Receptionist, take these to a detective down in Homicide but don't tell him where they came from.

Poor Julio.

"No, that won't work, Julio. The police will ask too many questions and your cousin could be in trouble. The best thing to do is to take these gloves with you and I'll pretend I never saw them."

"No way, Theo. They now belong to you." And with that, Julio jumped to his feet, grabbed the doorknob, and had one foot outside when he said, over his shoulder, "And you promised not to tell, Theo."

Theo was behind him. "Sure."

"You gave me your word."

"Sure."

Julio disappeared into the darkness.

CHAPTER
14

Judge devoured his bowl of spaghetti, but Theo hardly touched his. He put the dishes in the dishwasher, locked the house, and went to his room, where he changed into his pajamas, grabbed his laptop, and crawled into bed. He found April online and they chatted for a few minutes. She, too, was in bed, but her door was locked, as always. She was feeling much better. She and her mother had gone out for a pizza and even managed to laugh together. Her father was out of town, they thought, and that always made life easier. They said good night, and Theo closed his laptop and found the latest copy of *Sports Illustrated*. He couldn't read, couldn't concentrate. He was sleepy because he had not slept much the night before, and though he was worried and even frightened he soon nodded off.

Mr. Boone came home first. He crept up the stairs and opened the door to Theo's room. The door hinges squeaked, as always. He flipped on the light and smiled at the peaceful sight of his son fast asleep. "Good night, Theo," he whispered, and switched off the light.

The closing of the door awakened Theo, and within seconds he was lying on his back, staring at the dark ceiling, thinking about the golf gloves hidden in his office. There was something terribly wrong with Ike's advice to simply butt out, to ignore the existence of an eyewitness, and stand by quietly while the judicial system went haywire.

Yet, a promise is a promise, and Theo had given his word to Julio and to his cousin that he would keep their secret safe. What if he didn't? What if he marched into Judge Gantry's chambers first thing in the morning and flung the gloves on his desk and told everything? The cousin would be toast. He would be chased down by Jack Hogan and the police and hauled into custody. His testimony would save the day for the prosecution. A mistrial would be declared. A new trial would be scheduled. It would be all over the newspapers and television. The cousin would be the hero, but he would also be locked up as an illegal immigrant.

But couldn't he, the cousin, make a deal with the police and prosecutors? Wouldn't they cut him some slack because they needed him? Theo didn't know. Maybe, maybe not, but it was too risky.

Then he began thinking about Mrs. Duffy. In his file was a newspaper clipping with a nice photo of her. She was a very pretty woman, blond with dark eyes and perfect teeth. Imagine her final seconds as she realized with horror that her husband—wearing the two golf gloves—had not stopped by the house for some harmless reason, but instead was going for her throat.

Theo's heart was racing again. He threw the covers back and sat on the edge of his bed. Mrs. Duffy was only a few years younger than his mother. How would he feel if his mom were attacked in some savage manner?

If the jury found Mr. Duffy not guilty, he would literally get away with murder. And, he could never again be brought to trial for the crime. Theo knew all about double jeopardy—the State can't try you a second time if the jury finds you not guilty the first time. Since there were no more suspects, the murder would remain unsolved.

Mr. Duffy would collect his $1 million. Play even more golf. Probably find another pretty young wife.

Theo crawled back under the covers and tried to close

his eyes. He had an idea. After the trial, after Mr. Duffy was acquitted and drove away from the courthouse, Theo would wait a few weeks or months, then he would send the gloves to Mr. Duffy. Ship them in an anonymous package, maybe with a note that would read something like: "We know you killed her. And we're watching."

Why would he do that? He didn't know. Another foolish idea.

The thoughts became more random. There was no blood at the scene, right? So there would be no traces of blood on the gloves. But what about hair? What if a tiny strand of Mrs. Duffy's hair was somehow stuck to one of the gloves. Her hair was not short, certainly long enough to touch her shoulders. Theo had not dared open the plastic bag. He had not touched the gloves, so he didn't know what might be on them. A strand of hair would be even more proof that her husband killed her.

He tried to dwell on his spectacular victory in Animal Court on behalf of Hallie, his client and potential girlfriend. But his thoughts swung back to the crime scene. Finally, he grew still and fell asleep.

Marcella Boone arrived home just before 11:00 p.m. She checked the refrigerator to see what Theo had for dinner. She checked the dishwasher to make sure things were in order. She spoke to Woods, who was reading in the den. She climbed the stairs and woke up Theo for the second time in an hour. But he heard her coming and pretended to sleep through the ritual. She did not turn on the light, never did. She kissed him on the forehead, whispered, "Love you, Teddy," then left the room.

An hour later, Theo was wide awake, worrying about the hiding place he'd chosen for the gloves.

When the alarm on his cell phone buzzed at six thirty, Theo wasn't sure if he was awake or asleep, or somewhere in between, nor was he convinced he'd slept at all. He was fully aware, though, that he was tired and already irritable and facing another long day. The burden he carried was not normal for a thirteen-year-old.

His mother was at the stove—a rare spot for her—frying sausage and grilling pancakes, something she did about twice a year. Any other morning, Theo would've been starving and ready for a big breakfast. He didn't have the heart to tell her his appetite was gone.

"Did you sleep well, Teddy?" she asked as she pecked him on the cheek.

"Not really," he said.

"And why not? You look tired. Are you getting sick?"

"I'm fine."

"You need some orange juice. It's in the fridge."

They ate around the morning paper. "Looks like the trial is just about over," she said, her reading glasses halfway down her nose. She began most Fridays with a quick trip to the salon for work on her fingernails, so she was still in her bathrobe.

"I haven't kept up," Theo said.

"I don't believe that. Your eyes are red, Theo. You look tired."

"I said I didn't sleep well."

"Why not?"

Well, Dad woke me up at ten and you woke me up at eleven. But Theo couldn't blame his parents. He was losing sleep for other reasons. "A big test today," he said, and it was sort of true. Miss Garman had threatened them with a quiz in Geometry.

"You'll do fine," she said, and returned to the newspaper. "Eat your sausage."

He managed to choke down enough pancakes and sausage to satisfy her. He thanked her for the big breakfast, and as soon as possible he wished her a good day, said good-bye, gave a pat on the head to Judge, and took off on his bike. Ten minutes later he was racing up the steps to Ike's office, where his cranky uncle was waiting for the second early morning meeting in two days.

Ike looked even rougher on Friday. His eyes were puffy and redder than Theo's, and his wild gray hair had not been touched that morning. "This better be good," he growled.

"It is," Theo said as he stood in front of the desk.

"Have a seat."

"I'd rather stand."

"Okay. What's up?"

Theo unloaded the story about Julio and the two golf gloves in a plastic bag, now hidden behind some old Boone & Boone divorce files at the bottom of an old file cabinet in the basement where no one had ventured in at least a decade. He left nothing out of the story, except, of course, the identity of Julio and his cousin. He was finished in minutes.

Ike listened intently. He scratched his beard, took off his glasses, rubbed his eyes, sipped his coffee, and when Theo went silent Ike managed to mumble, "Unbelievable."

"What are we gonna do, Ike?" Theo asked in desperation.

"I don't know. The gloves need to be examined by the crime lab. They could have small samples of skin, Mrs.

Duffy's skin, or her hair, or they could even have DNA from Mr. Duffy's sweat."

Theo hadn't thought about the sweat.

"The gloves could be crucial evidence," Ike was saying, thinking out loud, still scratching his beard.

"We can't just ignore this, Ike. Come on."

"Why did you keep them?"

"I didn't really keep them, you know? It was more like my friend just left them. He's scared. His cousin is really scared. I'm scared. What are we gonna do?"

Ike stood and stretched and took another gulp of coffee. "Are you going to school?"

What else would I do on this Friday morning? "Sure. I'm already late."

"Go to school. I'll go watch the courthouse. I'll figure out something and I'll text you later."

"Thanks, Ike. You're the greatest."

"Don't know about that."

Theo walked into homeroom five minutes late, but Mr. Mount was in a good mood and the class had not exactly come to order. When he saw Theo, he pulled him aside and said, "Say, Theo, I was thinking that you could give us an update on the trial. Later, during Government."

The last thing Theo wanted to do was talk about the trial, but he could not say no to Mr. Mount. Plus, Mr. Mount was known to be a bit slack with his class preparations on Fridays, and he needed Theo to help fill in the gaps.

"Sure," Theo said.

"Thanks. Just an update, fifteen minutes or so. It goes to the jury today, right?"

"Probably so."

Theo took his seat. Mr. Mount tapped his desk, then called the roll. Announcements were made, the usual home-room routine. When the bell for first period rang, the boys headed for the door. A classmate named Woody followed Theo into the hall and grabbed him near the lockers. One look at his face, and Theo knew something was wrong.

"Theo, I need some help," Woody said quietly while glancing around. Woody's home life was chaotic. His parents were on their second or third marriages and there wasn't much supervision there. He played the electric guitar in a bad garage band, was already smoking, dressed like a runaway, and was rumored to have a small tattoo on his rear end. Theo, like the rest of the boys, was curious about the tattoo, but had no desire to confirm the rumor. In spite of all these distractions, Woody maintained a B average.

"What's up?" Theo asked. He really wanted to inform

Woody that this was a terrible time to ask for free legal advice. Theo had too much on his mind.

"You can keep this quiet, right?" Woody asked.

"Of course." Great. Just what Theo needed. Another secret.

Hallie walked by, slowed for a second, flashed a comely smile at Theo, but realized he was busy. She disappeared.

"My brother got arrested last night, Theo," Woody said, and his eyes were wet. "The police came to the house after midnight, took him away in handcuffs. It was terrible. He's in jail."

"What's the charge?"

"Drugs. Possession of pot, maybe distribution."

"There's a big difference between possession and distribution."

"Can you help us?"

"I doubt it. How old is he?"

"Seventeen."

Theo knew the brother by reputation, and it was not a good one. "First offense?" Theo asked, though he suspected the answer was no.

"He got busted for possession last year, his first. Slap on the wrist."

"Your parents need to hire a lawyer, Woody. It's that simple."

"Nothing's simple. My parents don't have the money, and if they did they wouldn't spend it on a lawyer. There's a war in my house, Theo. Kids against parents, and nobody's taking prisoners. My stepfather has been fighting with my brother over the drug thing, and he's promised a thousand times he will not get involved when the cops bust him."

The bell rang. The hall was empty.

Theo said, "Okay, catch me at recess. I don't have much advice, but I'll do what I can."

"Thanks, Theo."

They hustled into Madame Monique's class. Theo took his seat, opened his backpack, and realized he had not done his homework. At that moment, he really didn't care. At that moment, he was thankful he lived in a quiet and cozy home with great parents who seldom raised their voices. Poor Woody.

Then, he thought about the gloves.

CHAPTER 15

Halfway through Geometry, with Miss Garman still dropping hints about a quiz, and with Theo staring at the wall and trying to stay awake, the intercom above the door squawked and startled the class.

"Miss Garman, is Theo Boone in class?" It was the shrieking voice of Miss Gloria, the school's longtime secretary.

"He is," Miss Garman responded.

"Please send him down. He needs to check out."

Theo grabbed his things, stuffed them into his backpack, and as he was hustling toward the door Miss Garman said, "If we have a quiz, Theo, you can make it up on Monday."

Well, thanks for nothing, Theo thought, but instead he said, "Can't wait."

"Have a nice weekend, Theo," she said.

"You too."

He was in the hall before he took a breath and wondered who was checking him out, and for what reason. Maybe his mother had grown concerned about his red eyes and tired face and she had decided to take him to the doctor. Probably not. She was not one to overreact, and as a general rule she did not call the doctor until Theo was half dead. Maybe his father was having second thoughts and had decided to allow Theo to watch the last day of the trial. Probably not. Woods Boone was, as always, in another world.

Maybe it was something far worse. Some way, somehow, somebody had snitched on him and the police were waiting with a search warrant to find the gloves. The secrets would come out and he, Theo Boone, would find himself in serious trouble.

He slowed his pace. Where the hallway turned, he peeked through a large window and caught a glimpse of the front of the school. No police cars. Nothing to indicate trouble. He kept walking, even slower.

Ike was waiting. He was chatting with Miss Gloria when Theo entered the front office.

"This man says he's your uncle," Miss Gloria said with a smile.

"I'm afraid so," Theo said.

"And you have to go to a funeral over in Weeksburg?"

Ike was saying *Come on, Come on* with his eyes. Theo hesitated just for a second, then nodded and said, "I hate funerals."

"And you won't be coming back?" she said, reaching for a clipboard.

"No, the funeral is at one thirty," Ike said. "It'll kill the day."

"Sign here," she said.

Theo signed and they left the office. Ike's car was a Triumph Spitfire, a two-seater, at least thirty years old and far less than perfectly maintained. Like everything else in Ike's life, it was barely hanging together and lucky to be running.

They were a block from the school before Theo spoke. "A funeral, huh? I like it."

"It worked."

"And where are we going?"

"You've come to me for help. My advice is that we go to the offices of Boone and Boone, get your parents in a room, and tell them everything."

Theo took a deep breath. He couldn't argue. The issues involved were too complicated for him.

They surprised Elsa when they barged in the front door. She jumped to her feet and said, "Is something wrong?"

"Good morning, Elsa," Ike said. "You look exotic as always." She was wearing an orange sweater the color of a pumpkin with matching glasses and lipstick.

She ignored Ike, looked at Theo, and said, "What are you doing here?"

"I'm here for the funeral," Theo said, and began walking toward the library.

"Could you please round up Woods and Marcella?" Ike said. "We need to have a family meeting in the library."

Normally Elsa would have balked at being told what to do, but she knew this was serious. Luckily, Mrs. Boone was in her office, alone, and Mr. Boone was upstairs shoving paper around his desk. They hurried into the library, one after the other, and as soon as Ike closed the door Mrs. Boone looked at Theo and said, "Are you okay?" Mr. Boone looked at Theo and said, "What's going on here? Why aren't you in school?"

"Relax," Ike said. "Let's all have a seat and discuss

matters." They sat down, both parents eyeing Theo as if he'd committed a crime.

"Now," Ike continued, "Let me go first, then I'll shut up and Theo can talk. On Wednesday, just two days ago, Theo had a chat with one of his friends at school. This chat led to another chat, and in the course of these conversations Theo came across some information that could have a dramatic impact on the trial of Mr. Pete Duffy. In short, there's a witness out there, a witness no one knows about. Not the police, not the prosecution, not the defense, no one, except for Theo and his friend. Theo did not know what to do, so he came to me. I'm not sure what to do either, so here we are."

"Why didn't you tell us?" Mrs. Boone snapped.

"He's telling you now," Ike snapped back.

"I was scared," Theo said. "Still am, and I promised this friend that I would tell no one."

"What does this witness know?" asked Mr. Boone.

Theo looked at Ike and Ike looked at Theo. *Go ahead,* Ike said with his eyes. Theo cleared his throat and looked at his mother. "Well, this witness was in the woods near the Duffy home at the time of the murder. He saw Mr. Duffy pull up in a golf cart, take off his shoes, put a golf glove on his right hand, go inside the house, and come out a few minutes later. It was at the time of the murder. He put his shoes on, stuck the golf gloves in his bag, and sped away as if nothing happened."

"How do you know it was at the time of the murder?" Mrs. Boone asked.

"The pathologist testified that she died around eleven forty-five. The witness was on his lunch break, and it started at eleven thirty."

"And Mr. Duffy never saw this witness?" asked Mr. Boone.

"No. The man was hiding in the woods eating his lunch. He works at the golf course."

"Do you know his name?" Mrs. Boone asked.

"No, but I know who he is."

"Have you talked to him?" asked Mr. Boone.

"Yes."

"Where did you talk to him?" asked Mrs. Boone.

Theo felt like a trial witness suffering through a hot cross-examination. He hesitated, and Ike jumped back in. "He'd rather not divulge the names of the witness or the friend, and if you ask too many questions, then their identities might become obvious."

"I promised," Theo said, pleading. "In fact, I promised not to say a word to anyone. I don't know what to do."

"So he came to me first," Ike said. "For advice. He didn't want to trouble you, but now there's more to the story. Right, Theo?"

Both parents glared at him. Theo squirmed in his chair. He tapped his fingers on the long oak table.

"Go ahead, Theo," Ike said.

"Let's have it," Mr. Boone said.

Theo told them about the gloves.

"And you have them in your possession?" Mrs. Boone asked when he finished.

"Yes."

"Where are they now?"

"Downstairs, hidden behind a box of old divorce files."

"Downstairs, here? In our office?"

"Yes, Mom. Here. Below us."

Mr. Boone whistled and said, "Oh boy."

There was a long silence as the four Boones pondered the situation and tried to sort out which laws and which procedures might apply to this unusual set of facts. Though he'd said more than he planned to, Theo was relieved that his burden had now been shared. His parents would know what to do. Ike would offer some advice. Surely the three adults could figure this out.

"The paper said the trial might be over today," Mrs. Boone said.

"I just left the courtroom," Ike said. "Mr. Duffy is expected to testify this afternoon, and he's the last witness. After closing arguments, the jury will get the case."

"The gossip at the café this morning was that Judge Gantry will hold court tomorrow and wait for the jury," Mr. Boone said.

"On Saturday?"

"That was the gossip."

There was another long gap in the conversation. Mrs. Boone looked at her son and said, "Well, Theo, what do you suggest we do at this point?"

Theo was hoping the adults would know what to do. He squirmed a little, then said, "It seems to me that the best thing to do is to tell Judge Gantry the whole story."

"I agree," she said with a smile.

"Me too," said Ike.

It was no surprise, at least to Theo, that his father did not agree. "But what if we tell Judge Gantry," Mr. Boone said, "and he presses Theo for the name or identity of this witness? And Theo refuses to cough up the name? Then what? It could be that Judge Gantry holds him in contempt."

"I'm not sure what that means," Theo blurted.

"It means trouble," his father said.

"It means he could throw you in jail until you give him what he wants," Ike said with a nasty grin, as if he thought this was humorous.

"I'd rather not go to jail," Theo said.

"Don't be ridiculous, Woods," Mrs. Boone said. "Henry Gantry would not hold Theo in contempt."

"I'm not so sure about that," Woods fired back. "You have a crucial eyewitness whose testimony could potentially change the outcome of the trial, and you have one person who knows about this eyewitness. That person is Theo, and if he refuses to obey the judge, then the judge might get upset. I wouldn't blame him."

"I really don't want to go to jail," Theo said.

"You're not going to jail," Mrs. Boone said. "No judge in his right mind would lock up an innocent thirteen-year-old."

Another long pause.

Finally, Mr. Boone said, "Theo, what would happen if the identity of this witness were somehow revealed?"

"He's an illegal immigrant, Dad. He's not supposed to be here, and he's scared. If the police know his name and find him, then he's in jail and it's all my fault. If they don't catch him, then he'll disappear."

"Then don't tell us who he is," Mrs. Boone said.

"Thank you, Mom. I wasn't planning on it."

"Don't tell anyone."

"Got it. But now you know he's an illegal immigrant and he works at the golf course. He wouldn't be hard to find."

"And how did you get to know this person?" Mr. Boone asked.

"He has a cousin at school, and this cousin came to me for help."

"Like all the other kids at school," Ike said.

"Not all, but most of them."

Everyone took a deep breath, then Mr. Boone looked at Theo and smiled. "It's the family from the shelter, isn't it? Julio, your friend, the kid you tutor in math? And his mother, what's her name?"

"Carola," Theo's mother answered.

"Carola, right. I've spoken to her several times. She has two smaller kids, and Julio. They're from El Salvador. Julio's cousin is the mysterious eyewitness. Right, Theo?"

Theo nodded. Yes, Dad, you figured it out. And in an odd way he was relieved. He didn't actually betray a confidence, and someone had to know the truth.

CHAPTER
16

It occurred to Theo, as he walked behind his parents and Ike, that this was perhaps the first time he'd entered the courthouse with some reluctance. He was always excited to be there, to see the clerks and lawyers hustle about with their important matters, to take in the large, open marble foyer with an old chandelier hanging from above and massive portraits of dead judges on the walls. He'd always loved the courthouse, but such feelings of fondness were absent now. Theo was afraid of what was about to happen, though he had no idea what it might be.

They marched upstairs to the second floor, to the closed and guarded door of the main courtroom. A bailiff named Snodgrass informed them that the trial was in session and the door would not be opened until a recess. So they marched down the hall to the office of the Honorable Henry L. Gantry, where his secretary, Mrs. Irma Hardy, was typing away when they entered.

"Good morning, Irma," Mrs. Boone said.

"Well, good morning, Marcella, and Woods, and, well, hello, Theo." Mrs. Hardy was standing and removing her glasses and obviously uncertain as to why the entire Boone family had suddenly appeared at her desk. She looked suspiciously at Ike, as if their paths had crossed long ago under circumstances that had been less than ideal. Ike was wearing jeans, white sneakers, and a T-shirt, but thankfully, he'd put on an old brown blazer and it gave him some measure of credibility.

"Ike Boone," he said, thrusting out a hand. "Brother of Woods, uncle of Theo. Used to be a lawyer around here."

Mrs. Hardy managed a fake smile as if she remembered the name and shook his hand.

Mrs. Boone said, "Look, Irma, we have an urgent matter to discuss with Judge Gantry. I know he's on the bench right now, the Duffy trial, and, well, that's why we're here. I'm afraid it's crucial that we speak with him."

Mr. Boone barged in, "What time will he break for lunch?"

"Usually around noon, same as always, but he'll meet

with all the lawyers during lunch," Mrs. Hardy said, glancing at each of the four faces staring at her. "He's extremely busy, you know."

Theo looked at the large clock on the wall behind her. It was ten minutes after eleven.

"It's imperative that we see the judge as soon as possible," Mrs. Boone said, a bit too pushy in Theo's opinion. But then, she was a divorce lawyer and she was not known to be timid.

But this was Mrs. Hardy's turf and she was not one to be pushed around. "Well, it might be helpful if you tell me what's up," she said.

"I'm afraid it's confidential," Mr. Boone said with a frown.

"We simply can't do that, Irma, I'm sorry," Mrs. Boone added.

There were some chairs across the room, under yet more portraits of dead judges. Mrs. Hardy waved at them and said, "You may wait here. I'll inform the judge as soon as he breaks for lunch."

"Thank you, Irma," Mrs. Boone said.

"Thanks," Mr. Boone said.

Everyone took a breath, and smiled, and the Boones retreated.

"Theo, why aren't you in school?" Mrs. Hardy asked.

"It's a very long story," he said. "I'll tell you one day."

The four Boones sat down, and within fifteen seconds Ike was leaving, mumbling about going for a smoke. Mrs. Boone was on her cell phone, checking on some pressing matter with Elsa back at the office. Mr. Boone was poring over a document from a file he'd brought.

Theo remembered Woody and the arrest of his brother. He opened his backpack, removed his laptop, and began searching the Criminal Court dockets and arrest records. Such information was not available to the public online, but Theo, as always, used the Boone law firm's access code to find whatever he needed.

Woody's brother, Tony, was being held in the Strattenburg Juvenile Detention Center, the fancy name for the jail where they locked up those under the age of eighteen. Tony was charged with possession of marijuana with intent to sell, a crime that carried a maximum sentence of ten years in prison. Because he was seventeen, a minor, he could probably work a deal that would allow him to plead guilty and serve two years in another youth facility. Assuming, of course, he agreed to plead guilty. If he wanted to plead not guilty, then he would face a jury and run the risk of a much longer sentence. Juveniles charged with drug violations went to trial in less than 2 percent of the cases.

If the parents and stepparents refused to help, as Woody

had said, then his brother would be assigned to a public defender. In Strattenburg, the public defenders were very good and handled similar drug cases every day.

Theo quickly summarized this in an e-mail and zipped it to Woody. He sent another e-mail to Mr. Mount and explained that he was not at school and would miss Government. He sent a quick Hello to April.

The clock on the wall seemed to freeze. Mrs. Hardy was busy with her typing. All the dead judges seemed to stare down at Theo, none of them smiling, all somber-faced and suspicious, as if to say, "Son, what are you doing here?" His father was out in the hall, on the phone, dealing with some crucial real estate matter. His mother was on her laptop, pecking away as if lives were at stake. Ike was still by a window somewhere, blowing smoke out of the building.

Theo wandered off. He climbed the stairs and stopped by the Family Court office where he hoped to find Jenny, but she was not there. He drifted down to Animal Court, but the room was empty. Then he climbed an old, dark stairwell, the one no one used and few people even knew about, and silently made his way through a dimly lit hallway on the third floor until he came to an abandoned room that had once housed the county law library. It was used for storage and packed with boxes of old land records and outdated computers. A thick layer of dust covered everything, and Theo left footprints on the floor as he tiptoed through the rubble. He opened the door to a small closet, then closed the door behind him. The space was so dark he could not see his hands. Near the floor was a crack, a sliver of an opening, and through it Theo could see the courtroom below. His view was from high above, over the heads of the jurors.

It was a splendid view, one that Theo had discovered himself a year earlier when a crime victim testified in a case so horrible that Judge Gantry cleared the courtroom. Her testimony made Theo ill and he'd wished a thousand times that he had not spied on the trial. From inside the courtroom, the crack in the paneling could not be seen. It was just above a row of thick velvet curtains above the jury box.

One of Mr. Duffy's golfing buddies was on the witness stand, and though Theo could not hear well he got the gist of the testimony. The witness was explaining that Mr. Duffy was a serious golfer, who, for several years now, had often played alone. This was not unusual. Many golfers, especially the more serious ones, like to work on their game by playing alone.

The courtroom was packed. Theo could not see the

balcony, but he guessed it was crowded, too. He had a clear shot at Mr. Duffy, who sat among his lawyers at the defense table. He looked confident, almost certain that the trial was playing out in his favor and that the jury would find him not guilty.

Theo watched for a few minutes, then the lawyers started yelling and he slipped out of the closet. He was halfway down the stairwell when he saw something move on the landing below. Someone was down there, in the shadows, hiding. Theo froze and got a whiff of something burning. The man was smoking a cigarette, which was against the rules because they were still inside the building. He blew a huge cloud, then stepped onto the landing. It was Omar Cheepe, visible now with his massive slick head and black eyes. He looked up at Theo, said nothing, then turned and walked away.

Theo did not know if he'd been followed, or if the stairwell was one of Omar's smoking places. There were cigarette butts everywhere. Maybe others sneaked down there for a smoke. A voice told him, though, that the encounter was not an accident.

It was almost 1:00 p.m. when Judge Gantry yanked open the door to his office and walked straight to the Boones as they sat like naughty schoolchildren waiting in the principal's office. He wore no robe, no jacket, just a white shirt with the sleeves rolled up, the tie loosened, the look of a man hard at work and under pressure. He did not smile and was clearly irritated.

The Boones jumped to their feet. There were no Hellos or greetings of any nature. Judge Gantry just said, "This better be good."

"Sorry, Judge," Mr. Boone managed to say first. "We understand what's happening right now and realize the strain you're under."

"Our apologies, Henry," Mrs. Boone added quickly. "But it's a crucial matter that might impact this trial."

By calling him Henry instead of Judge or something more formal, Mrs. Boone managed to cool things a bit. Regardless of how irritated the judge might appear, she was not the least bit intimidated.

"Just five minutes," she added as she picked up her purse.

Judge Gantry glared at Theo as if he'd just shot someone, then he looked at Ike, managed a brief smile, and said, "Hello, Ike. It's been a long time."

"Yes it has, Henry," Ike said.

The smile was gone, and Judge Gantry said, "You have five minutes."

They quickly followed him back into his office, and as the door was closing Theo glanced back at Mrs. Irma Hardy. She was typing away, as if she had no interest in what was about to be discussed. Theo figured she would know everything within half an hour.

The four Boones lined up in chairs on one side of a long worktable in one corner of the huge office. Judge Gantry faced them on the other. Theo sat between his parents, and though he was quite nervous he also felt well-protected.

His mother went first. "Henry, we have reason to believe that there is a witness to the murder of Myra Duffy. A witness who is hiding. A witness unknown to the police, the prosecutors, and certainly to the defense."

"May I ask why Theo is in the middle of this?" the judge asked, his eyebrows arched and twitching. "Seems to me he should be in school right about now. This is not exactly a matter for a child."

First, Theo actually preferred to be in school at that moment. Second, the use of the word *child* really irritated him. Theo said, slowly, "Because, Judge, I know who the witness is. They don't, but I do."

Judge Gantry's eyes were red and he looked very tired. He exhaled, a long, impressive release of air, much like an inner tube finally being relieved of too much pressure. The thick wrinkles in his forehead flattened and relaxed. He asked, "And what's your role in all this, Ike?"

"Oh, I'm just Theo's legal adviser." Ike thought it was funny but the humor was lost on the rest of them.

A pause, then, "Okay, why don't we start at the beginning? I'd like to know what this witness allegedly saw. Who can tell me this?"

"I can," Theo said. "But I promised I would never reveal his name."

"You promised this to whom?"

"To the witness."

"So you've talked to this witness?"

"Yes, sir."

"And you believe he's telling the truth?"

"I do, yes, sir."

Another release of air. Another rub of the eyes. "All right, Theo. I'm listening. Please move things along."

Theo told the story.

When he finished, the room was silent. Judge Gantry slowly reached over to a phone on the table, pushed a button, and said, "Mrs. Hardy, please inform the bailiff that I will be delayed for thirty minutes. Keep the jurors in the jury room."

A crisp voice answered, "Yes, sir."

He fell back into his chair. All four Boones watched him but he avoided their gaze.

"And you have the gloves?" he said, his voice much lower, much calmer.

"They're in our office," Mr. Boone said. "We'll be happy to hand them over."

Judge Gantry raised both hands, both palms visible. "No, no. Not yet anyway. Maybe later, maybe never. Just let me think for a moment." And with that, he slowly got to his feet and walked to the window behind his massive desk at the other end of the room. He stood there for a moment, looking out, though there wasn't much of a view. He seemed to forget that just down the hall there was a courtroom full of people and they were all anxiously waiting on him.

"Did I do okay?" Theo whispered to his mother. She smiled, patted his arm, and said, "Nice job, Teddy. Smile."

The judge was back, in his chair, across the table. He looked at Theo and asked, "Why won't this person come forward?"

Theo hesitated because if he said too much more, he might compromise the identity of Julio's cousin. Ike decided to help. "Judge, the witness is an illegal immigrant, one of many around here. He's skittish right now, and you can't blame him. Any whiff of trouble, and he'll vanish into the underground and be gone forever."

Theo added, "He thinks he'll be arrested if he comes forward."

Ike added, "And Theo promised the guy he wouldn't tell a soul."

Mr. Boone added, "But he thinks it's important to inform the court that a crucial witness is missing from the trial."

Mrs. Boone added, "While at the same time protecting the identity of the witness."

"All right, all right," Judge Gantry said, and glanced at his watch. "I can't stop the trial at this point. We're almost ready for the jury to begin deliberations. If a surprise witness appeared now, it would be difficult to stop the trial and allow him to testify. And we don't even have a surprise witness. We have a phantom witness. I can't stop the trial."

These words echoed around the room and fell heavily onto the table. All Theo could think about was Mr. Duffy sitting with all his lawyers, smug and confident that he was about to get away with murder.

"Judge, can I make a suggestion?" Ike asked.

"Sure, Ike. I could use some help."

"Gossip is that you're going to hold court tomorrow, on Saturday, and wait on a verdict."

"That's right."

"Why not send the jury home until Monday, like most trials? Bring them back Monday morning to start their deliberations. This is a trial, not emergency surgery. Things aren't that urgent."

"So what's your plan?"

"I don't have one. But it would give us some time to think about this witness, maybe find a way to help him. I don't know. It just seems wrong to rush to a verdict, especially a verdict that might be wrong."

"Wrong?"

"Yes. I've watched some of the trial. I've watched the jurors. The State started with a weak case and it's gotten even weaker. Pete Duffy is about to walk."

Judge Gantry nodded slightly, as if he agreed, but he said nothing. He began getting ready. He buttoned his cuffs, adjusted his tie, stood and reached for his black robe hanging near the door.

"I'll think about it," he said, finally. "Thank you for your, uh . . ."

"Intrusion," said Mr. Boone with a laugh. The Boones were pushing back and standing up.

"No, not at all, Woods. This presents a unique situation, something I've never encountered before. But then, every trial is different. Thank you, Theo."

"Yes, Your Honor."

"Are you watching the rest of the trial?"

"We can't get a seat," Theo said.

"Well, let me see what I can do about that."

CHAPTER
17

O nce the jurors had taken their seats and the courtroom was quiet and all eyes were on Judge Gantry, he said, "Mr. Nance, I believe you have one more witness."

Clifford Nance stood, straight and important, and said, with drama, "Your Honor, the defense calls Mr. Peter Duffy himself."

The tension was suddenly thick as the defendant made his way to the witness chair. Finally, after four long days of trial, the accused would take the stand and tell his side of the story. But, in doing so he would also subject himself to questions from the prosecution. Theo knew that in 65 percent of murder cases the defendant does not testify, and he knew the reasons why. First, they're usually guilty of the murder and cannot withstand a clever and nasty cross-examination from the prosecution. Second, they usually have a record of prior criminal activity, and once on the witness stand the record becomes fair game. In every trial the judge tries to explain to the jury that the defendant does not have to testify, does not have to say a word nor produce any witnesses on his behalf. The burden is on the State to prove him guilty.

Theo also knew that jurors are very suspicious of a defendant who will not testify to save his own neck. If they were suspicious of Pete Duffy, Theo could not tell. They watched him closely as he settled into the witness chair, raised his right hand, and swore to tell the truth.

Theo could see it all because, thanks to Judge Gantry, he was sitting in a ringside seat in the second row, behind the defense, with Ike to his right and his father to his left. His mother had appointments back at the office. She said she couldn't *waste* the afternoon sitting through a trial, though it was obvious to the other three Boones that she really wanted to.

Clifford Nance cleared his throat and asked the defendant to state his name, a necessary but rather silly thing to do under the circumstances. Everyone in the courtroom not only knew Pete Duffy, but also knew a lot about him. Mr. Nance then began a series of simple questions. He took his time establishing the basics—Mr. Duffy's family history, education, jobs, businesses, lack of criminal record, and so on. The two had spent hours rehearsing all this, and the witness settled into a routine. He often glanced over at the jurors in an effort to establish an easy conversational tone. *Trust me,* he seemed to be trying to say. He was a nice-looking man in a stylish suit, and this struck Theo as a little odd because none of the five male jurors wore a coat or a tie. Theo had read articles about the strategy of what lawyers and their clients should wear during a trial.

The back-and-forth finally got around to something important when Mr. Nance brought up the subject of the $1 million insurance policy on the life of Mrs. Myra Duffy. The witness explained that he was a firm believer in life insurance, that when he was a young man with a young wife and young children he had always saved his money and invested in life insurance, both for himself and for his wife. Life policies are valuable tools to protect a family in the event of an untimely death. Later, when he married his second wife, Myra, he had insisted on purchasing life insurance. And Myra agreed. In fact, the $1 million policies had actually been her idea. She wanted the protection in case something happened to him.

Though he seemed unable to completely relax, Mr. Duffy was believable. The jurors listened carefully. So did Theo, and more than once he reminded himself that he was watching the biggest trial in Strattenburg's history. Plus, he was also skipping school, with an excuse.

From the life insurance, Mr. Nance moved the conversation to Mr. Duffy's business ventures. And here, the witness scored well. He admitted that some of his real estate deals had gone sour, that some of the banks were squeezing him, that he'd lost a few partners and made some mistakes. His humility was touching and well received by the jurors. It made him even more believable. He strongly denied that he was even remotely close to bankruptcy, and rattled off an impressive series of steps he was taking to unload debt and save his assets.

Some of it was over Theo's head, and he suspected a few of the jurors were slightly confused, too. It didn't matter. Clifford Nance had his client thoroughly prepared.

Under the State's theory, the motive for the killing was money and greed. This theory was looking weaker and weaker.

Mr. Nance then moved to the delicate matter of the Duffys' marital troubles, and here again the witness did a fine job. He admitted things had been rocky. Yes, they had gone to marriage counselors. Yes, they had consulted separate divorce lawyers. Yes, there had been fights, but none violent. And yes, he had moved out on one occasion, a miserable one-month period that made him even more determined to patch things up. At the time she was killed, they were together and happy and making plans for the future.

Another whack at the prosecution's theory.

As the afternoon wore on, Clifford Nance steered the testimony to the subject of golf, and there they spent a lot of time. Too much time, in Theo's humble opinion. Mr. Duffy was adamant in his assertions that he had always preferred to play golf alone and had been doing so for decades. Mr. Nance produced a file and explained to the judge that it contained his client's scorecards that dated back twenty years. He handed one to the witness, who identified it. It was from a golf course in California, fourteen years earlier. He had shot an eighty-one, nine over par. He'd played alone.

One scorecard followed another, and the testimony soon became a tour of golf courses all over the United States. Pete Duffy played a lot of golf! He was serious. He kept his records. And he played alone. He went on to explain that he also played with friends, played for business, even played with his son every chance he got. But he preferred to play alone, on an empty course.

When the tour was over, there seemed little doubt that another of the prosecution's theories had been shot down. The notion that Pete Duffy had been planning the murder for two years, and that he began playing golf alone so he could pull it off with no witnesses around, seemed unlikely.

Theo kept thinking: There are four people in this crowded courtroom who know the truth. Me, Ike, my dad, and Pete Duffy. We know he killed his wife.

Ike kept thinking: This guy's about to walk and there's nothing we can do. It's the perfect crime.

Woods Boone kept thinking: How can we find the mysterious witness and bring him in before it's too late?

The last scorecard was from the day of the murder. Mr. Duffy had played eighteen holes, shot six over par, and played alone. Of course, the scorecard had been kept by him, so its accuracy could be questioned.

(Theo had already learned that, in golf, most scorecards reflect something other than the actual number of strokes.)

Mr. Nance became much more somber when he questioned his client about the day of the murder, and his client responded well. Mr. Duffy's voice grew quieter, sort of scratchy and pained as he talked about his wife's brutal death.

I wonder if he's going to cry, Theo was asking himself, though he was moved by the testimony.

Pete Duffy held off the tears and did a superb job of describing the horror of hearing the news, racing home in his golf cart, and finding the police there. His wife's body had not been moved, and when he saw her he collapsed and had to be assisted by a detective. Later, he was seen by a doctor and given some medication.

What a liar, Theo thought. What a phony. You killed your wife. There is a witness. I have your gloves hidden at the office.

Pete Duffy talked about the nightmare of calling her family, his family, their friends, and planning and enduring the funeral and burial. The loneliness. The emptiness of living in the same house where his dear wife had been murdered. The thoughts of selling it and moving away. The daily trips to the cemetery.

Then, the horror of being suspected, accused, indicted, arrested, and put on trial. How could anyone suspect him in the murder of a woman he loved and adored?

He finally broke down. He struggled to control himself and wiped his eyes and repeatedly said, "I'm sorry, I'm sorry." It was very moving, and Theo watched the faces of the jurors. Total sympathy and belief. Duffy was crying to save his life, and it was working.

As his client tried to regain his composure, Clifford Nance decided they had scored enough. He announced, "No more questions, Your Honor. We tender the witness."

Mr. Jack Hogan stood immediately and said, "May I suggest a short recess, Your Honor?" A recess would break the action, take the jurors away from the emotional testimony they had just heard. And, it was just after three thirty. Everyone needed a break.

"Fifteen minutes," Judge Gantry said. "Then we'll start the cross-examination."

Fifteen minutes dragged into thirty. "He's running out the clock," Ike said. "It's Friday afternoon. Everyone's tired. He'll send the jury home and come back Monday."

"I don't know," said Woods Boone. "He might want the final arguments this afternoon."

They were huddled in the hallway, near the soft drink machines. Other little groups of spectators were waiting, watching the clocks on the wall. Omar Cheepe appeared and needed something to drink. He put some coins in a machine, made his selection while glancing at the Boones, then retrieved the can from the dispenser.

Ike kept talking. "Hogan won't touch him. He's too slick."

"The jury will find him not guilty in less than an hour," Woods said.

"He's walking," Theo added.

"I really need to get back to the office," Woods said.

"So do I," Ike added. Typical Boones.

Neither made a move because both wanted to see the end of the trial. Theo was just glad they were together and having a discussion, a rarity.

There was movement down the hall, and the crowd began to shuffle toward the courtroom. A few had left during the recess. It was, after all, Friday afternoon.

When they were inside and seated again, and quiet, Judge Gantry assumed his position on the bench and nodded at Jack Hogan. It was time for the cross-examination, and when a defendant was on the stand and a prosecutor had the right to question him aggressively, the result was usually pretty ugly.

Jack Hogan walked to the witness stand and handed Pete Duffy a document. "Recognize this, Mr. Duffy?" Hogan asked, suspicion dripping from every syllable.

Duffy took his time, looked it over, front and back, for several pages. "Yes," he finally said.

"Please tell the jury what it is?"

"It's a foreclosure notice."

"On which property?"

"Rix Road Shopping Center."

"Here in Strattenburg?"

"Yes."

"And the Rix Road Shopping Center is owned by you?"

"Yes, me and a partner."

"And the bank sent you that foreclosure notice in September of last year because you were behind in the quarterly payments on the mortgage. Is that correct?"

"That's what the bank said."

"Do you disagree, Mr. Duffy? Are you telling this jury that you were not behind in the mortgage payments on this property in September of last year?" Jack Hogan waved some more papers as he asked this, as if he had plenty of proof.

Duffy paused, then offered a fake grin. "Yes, we were behind in the payments."

"And the bank had loaned you how much money on this property?"

"Two hundred thousand dollars."

"Two hundred thousand dollars," Hogan repeated as he looked at the jurors. Then he walked to his table, put down one handful of papers and picked up another. He situated himself behind the podium and said, "Now, Mr. Duffy, did you own a warehouse on Wolf Street in the industrial park here in Strattenburg?"

"Yes, sir. I had two partners in that deal."

"And you sold the warehouse, didn't you?"

"Yes, we sold it."

"And the sale took place last September, right?"

"If you say so. I'm sure you have the paperwork."

"Indeed I do. And my paperwork shows that the warehouse was on the market for over a year, that the asking price was six hundred thousand dollars, the mortgage at State Bank was five hundred fifty, and that you and your partners finally sold it for just over four hundred thousand." Hogan was sort of thrusting the paperwork in the air as he spoke. "You agree, Mr. Duffy?"

"That sounds about right."

"So you lost a chunk of money on that deal, right, Mr. Duffy?"

"It was not one of my better deals."

"Were you desperate to sell the warehouse?"

"No."

"Did you need the cash, Mr. Duffy?"

The witness shifted weight and seemed a bit uncomfortable. "We, my partners and I, needed to sell the warehouse."

For the next twenty minutes, Hogan hammered away at

Pete Duffy and his partners and their financial woes. Duffy refused to admit that he had been *desperate*. But, as the cross-examination grew stressful, it became obvious that the witness had been scrambling to prop up one deal while another fell through. Hogan had plenty of paperwork. He produced copies of two lawsuits that had been filed against Pete Duffy by ex-partners. He grilled the witness about the allegations in the lawsuits. Duffy adamantly denied he was at fault and explained that neither case had merit. He freely admitted that his business had been struggling, but clung to the position that he had been far from bankruptcy.

Jack Hogan did a masterful job of portraying Duffy as a cash-starved wheeler-dealer who barely managed to stay one step ahead of his creditors. But linking his problems to the motive for murder was still a stretch.

Changing subjects, Hogan began to position himself for another bomb. He politely poked around the issue of the Duffys' troubled marriage, and after a few easy questions, asked, "Now, Mr. Duffy, you testified that you actually moved out, is that correct?"

"It is."

"And this separation lasted for one month?"

"I wouldn't call it a separation. We never referred to it as that."

"Then what was it called?"

"We didn't bother to give it a name, sir."

"Fair enough. When did you move out?"

"I didn't keep a journal, but it was July of last year."

"Roughly three months before her murder?"

"Something like that."

"Where did you live after you moved out?"

"I'm not sure I actually moved, sir. I just took some clothes and left."

"Okay, and where did you go?"

"I spent a few nights at the Marriott, just down the street. I spent a few nights with one of my partners. He's divorced and lives alone. It was a pretty lousy month."

"So you were just here and there? For about a month?"

"That's right."

"Then you moved back home, patched things up with Mrs. Duffy, and were in the process of living happily ever after when she was murdered?"

"Is that a question?"

"Strike it. Here's a question for you, Mr. Duffy." Jack Hogan was back with the paperwork. He handed a document to the witness, and with one glance Pete Duffy became pale.

"Recognize that, Mr. Duffy?"

"Uh, I'm not sure," Duffy said, flipping a page, trying to stall.

"Well, allow me to help. That's a four-page lease for an apartment over in Weeksburg, thirty miles away. The lease is for a nice, two-bedroom furnished apartment in a swanky building, two thousand dollars a month. Ring a bell, Mr. Duffy?"

"Not really. I, uh—"

"A one-year lease, beginning last June."

Duffy shrugged as if he had no clue. "It's not signed by me."

"No, but by your secretary, a Mrs. Judith Maze, a woman who's lived with her husband at the same address here in Strattenburg for the past twenty years. Right, Mr. Duffy?"

"If you say so. She is my secretary."

"Why would she sign a lease for such an apartment?"

"I have no idea. Maybe you should ask her."

"Mr. Duffy, do you really want me to call her as a witness?"

"Uh, sure. Go ahead."

"Have you ever seen this apartment, Mr. Duffy?"

Duffy was rattled and dazed and clinging to a slippery slope. He glanced at the jury box, offered another fake smile, then replied, "Yes, I've stayed there a couple of times."

"Alone?" Hogan barked with perfect timing and great suspicion.

"Of course I was alone. I was over there on business, things ran late, so I stayed in the apartment."

"How convenient. Who's paying the rent?"

"I don't know. You'll have to ask Mrs. Maze."

"So you're telling the jury, Mr. Duffy, that you did not lease this apartment and you're not paying the rent?"

"That's correct."

"And you've only stayed there a couple of times?"

"That's correct."

"And the leasing of this apartment had nothing to do with the problems you and Mrs. Duffy were having?"

"No. Again, I didn't lease the apartment."

To Theo, who knew the truth, Pete Duffy's honesty had been severely questioned. It seemed obvious that he was lying about the apartment. And if he told one lie, then he would certainly tell another.

Evidently, Jack Hogan had no way to prove how often Duffy had used the apartment. He moved on, to the subject of golf, and his cross-examination lost its steam. Duffy knew much more about golf than the prosecutor, and the two haggled and bickered for what seemed like an hour.

It was almost 6:00 p.m. when Jack Hogan finally sat

down. Judge Gantry wasted no time before announcing, "I have decided not to hold court tomorrow. I think the jurors need a break. I hope you have a quiet and restful weekend, and I'll see you here at nine Monday morning. At that time, we will have closing arguments, then you will finally get the case. Again, the usual instructions. Do not discuss this case. If anyone contacts you and attempts to discuss this case, please notify me immediately. Thank you for your service. I'll see you Monday."

The bailiffs escorted the jurors through a side door. Once they were gone, Judge Gantry looked at the lawyers and said, "Gentlemen, anything more?"

Jack Hogan stood and said, "Nothing at this time, Your Honor."

Clifford Nance stood and shook his head no.

"Very well. This court is adjourned until nine Monday morning."

CHAPTER 18

For the first time in several nights, Theo slept well. He awoke late on Saturday morning, and by the time he and Judge staggered downstairs he was aware that a family meeting of some variety was under way in the kitchen. His father was at the stove scrambling eggs. His mother, still in her night robe, sat at one end of the table pecking at a keyboard and studying the monitor. And Ike, who, to Theo's knowledge, had not been present in the house during the thirteen years Theo had been on the Earth, sat at the other end with the morning newspaper spread out before him. He was studying the classified ads and making notes. He was wearing a faded orange jogging suit and an old Yankees cap. The air was thick with the smell of breakfast and of conversations interrupted and unfinished. Judge went straight to the stove and began his usual routine of begging for food.

Various versions of Good Morning were exchanged. Theo walked to the stove and looked at the food. "All eggs are scrambled," his father said. His father cooked even less than his mother and the eggs looked a bit raw, at least in Theo's opinion. He poured himself some grapefruit juice and took a seat at the table.

No one spoke until Ike said, "Here's a two-bedroom garage apartment on Millmont. Six hundred a month. That's not a bad part of town."

"Millmont's okay," Mr. Boone said.

"She makes seven dollars an hour and works thirty hours a week," Mrs. Boone said, without looking up. "After taxes and a few necessities, she'll be lucky to have three hundred dollars a month for rent. She can't afford it. That's why they're living in the shelter."

"So where do you think we'll find an apartment for three hundred bucks a month?" Ike asked with a slight edge to his voice. He did not look up, though. In fact, at the moment no one was making eye contact with anyone else.

Theo just listened and watched.

_oone said, "If it's a garage apartment, then it's probably a single owner. I doubt if they'll rent to El Salvadorans or anyone else who's not from here." He thumped some eggs on a plate, added a toasted wheat muffin, and slid it in front of Theo, who quietly said, "Thanks." Judge finally got some eggs in his bowl.

Theo took a bite, chewed slowly, listened to the silence. Their disinterest in his involvement in whatever they were discussing irritated him. The eggs were too mushy.

He finally said, "Apartment hunting, are we?"

Ike managed to grunt, "Uh-huh."

El Salvadorans. Living at the shelter. The clues were adding up.

"Woods," Mrs. Boone said, still pecking. "Nick Wetzel advertises for immigration work. Is he a reputable lawyer? I've never met him."

"He advertises a lot," Mr. Boone replied. "He used to be on television begging for car wrecks. I'd stay away."

"Well, only two lawyers in town mention immigration work in their ads," she said.

"Talk to both of them," Ike said.

"I suppose so," she said.

"What are we doing here?" Theo finally asked.

"We have a busy day, Theo," his father said as he sat

down with a cup of coffee. "You and I have a very important golf game."

Theo couldn't suppress a smile. They played almost every Saturday, but for the past several days Theo had forgotten about his game. He, along with the rest of the town, had assumed that the trial would continue into Saturday and he certainly planned to be in the courtroom.

"Great. When?"

"We should leave in about thirty minutes."

Thirty minutes later they were putting their clubs into the back of Mr. Boone's SUV and talking about how beautiful the weather was. It was mid-April, no clouds, temperature expected to reach seventy degrees, the azaleas were blooming, and the neighbors were toiling away in their flower beds.

After a few minutes, Theo said, "Dad, where are we going?" It was obvious they were not headed to the Strattenburg Municipal Course, the only place they'd ever played.

"We're checking out a new course today."

"Which one?" Theo knew of only three in the area.

"Waverly Creek."

Theo allowed this to sink in, then said, "Awesome, Dad. The scene of the crime."

"Something like that. I have a client who lives out there and he invited us to play. He won't be around, though. Just the two of us. We'll play the Creek Course, so maybe there won't be a crowd."

Ten minutes later, they pulled into the rather grand entrance of Waverly Creek. A massive stone wall lined the road and disappeared around a bend. Heavy gates stopped all traffic. A man in a uniform stepped out of the guardhouse and approached them as Mr. Boone came to a stop and lowered his window.

"Good morning," the guard said, with a smile and a clipboard.

"Good morning. Name's Woods Boone. Here to play a little golf. Tee time at ten forty. Guests of Max Kilpatrick."

The guard studied his notes, then said, "Welcome, Mr. Boone. Put this on your dash." He handed over a bright yellow card and said, "Hit 'em straight."

"Thanks," Mr. Boone said, and the gates began to open.

Theo had been through them once before, a couple of years earlier, for the birthday party of a friend who had since moved away. He remembered the large homes, long driveways, fancy cars, and front lawns perfectly landscaped. They drove along a narrow road shaded with old trees, and passed a few fairways and greens. The course was manicured, like something out of a golf magazine. At every tee there were golfers taking practice swings and on every green there were more bent over their putters. Theo began to fret. He liked nothing more than eighteen holes with his dad on an uncrowded course, yet nothing was more unpleasant than trying to hit a ball with a foursome waiting and watching impatiently from behind.

The clubhouse was busy. Dozens of golfers were out on this fine day. Mr. Boone checked in with the starter, got a cart, and they began limbering up at the practice range. Theo couldn't help but look around, hoping to catch a glimpse of Julio's cousin. Or maybe he just might see Pete Duffy himself, out for a few holes with some friends after a rough week in court. He had posted bond the day of his arrest and had never been near a jail cell.

And, the way the trial was going, he was unlikely to be locked up.

But Theo saw neither man. The fact that he was thinking about them meant that he was not thinking about his golf swing. He sprayed a few balls around the range, and began to worry about his game.

They teed off on time, Mr. Boone from the blue tees, Theo from the whites, a little farther down the fairway. His drive was a line shot that barely covered a hundred yards.

"Keep your head down," his father said as they sped away in the cart. There would be more advice as the day progressed. Mr. Boone had been playing for thirty years and was an average golfer, and like most golfers he often could not resist the urge to give advice, especially to his son. Theo took it well. He needed lots of help.

There was a foursome in front of them and no one behind. The Creek Course was shorter, narrower, and therefore, less favored by the other golfers. It was designed to sort of follow the winding route of Waverly Creek, a pretty but treacherous little stream known to devour golf balls. The North Nine and South Nine were crowded, but not the Creek Course.

As they sat in the cart by the tee box and waited for the foursome to putt out on number three, Mr. Boone said, "Okay, Theo, here's the plan. Ike is looking for an apartment for the Pena family. Something small and affordable. If they need a little help with the rent, then your mother and I can kick in some money. This is something we've been talking about for several months, so it's nothing new. Ike, who's got a big heart but a small bank account, is willing to help, too. If we can find a place real fast, then maybe Carola can convince her nephew, Julio's cousin, to live with them. It will be a much more stable environment for all of them.

Ike is searching right now. And your mother is talking to immigration attorneys. There might be a way, under federal law, to allow an illegal immigrant to become legal if he has a sponsor who is a U.S. citizen, and if he has a job. Let's hit."

They teed off, got back in the cart, and eased along the cart path. Both drives were in the rough.

Mr. Boone continued as he drove. "Your mother and I are willing to sponsor Julio's cousin. I can probably find him a better job, a legitimate one, and if he lives with his aunt and her family he can probably obtain legal status within two years. Full citizenship is another matter."

"What's the catch?" Theo asked.

"There's no real catch. We want to help the Pena family get out of the shelter, and we'll do so regardless of what happens to the cousin. But we have to convince him to come forward and be willing to testify, to tell the truth, to take the witness stand and tell the jury what he saw."

"And how do we convince him to do that?"

"That part of the plan is still evolving."

Theo's ball was near the cart path, a nice distance off the fairway. He hit a five iron well and put the ball fifty yards from the green.

"Nice shot, Theo."

"I get lucky every now and then."

Number six was a dogleg to the left, a wider fairway with beautiful homes along the right-hand boundary. From the tee box, they could see the rear of the Duffy home 150 yards down the cart path. Next door to it, a gardener was busy mowing grass. Theo thought, The way I'm hitting, that man's in danger.

But the gardener was not injured after both Boones teed off. They crept along the cart path. Mr. Boone said, "You told me you had aerial maps of this place."

"Yes, sir. At the office."

"You think you can find the spot where our witness was hiding?"

"Maybe. It's over there." Theo pointed to a patch of thick trees across the fairway. They drove to the edge of the woods, got out, and began stomping around like golfers do when they've hit bad shots and can't find their balls. A dry creek bed ran through the woods, and on one side there was a short retaining wall of eight-by-eight treated timbers. The perfect spot to sit and hide and have a quiet lunch, all alone.

"That might be it," Theo said, pointing. "He said he was sitting on some logs, with a perfect view of the house."

Theo and Mr. Boone sat on the timbers. The view of the rear of the Duffy house was unobstructed. "How far away, you think?" asked Theo.

"A hundred yards," Mr. Boone said without hesitation, the way most golfers readily estimate distances. "It's a great hiding place. No one would ever see him sitting here. No one would ever think to look in these trees."

"When you study the aerial, you can see the maintenance shed just over there, through the woods." Theo was pointing in the other direction, opposite the fairway. "According to the cousin, the workers meet for lunch at eleven thirty at the shed. On most days, he slipped away to eat by himself. I guess he came here."

"I brought a camera. Let's take some photos." Mr. Boone retrieved a small digital camera from his golf bag on the cart. He photographed the wooded area, the creek bed, the retaining wall, then turned and took some of the fairway and the homes on the other side.

"What are the photos for?" Theo asked when they were back in the cart.

"We might need them."

They took photos for a few minutes, then emerged from the woods and were almost to the golf cart when Theo looked across the fairway. Pete Duffy was standing on his patio, watching them through binoculars. There were no other golfers around. "Dad," Theo said softly.

"I see him," Mr. Boone replied. "Let's hit."

They tried to ignore him as they hit their second shots, neither of which landed anywhere near the green. They quickly hopped in the cart and drove away. Pete Duffy never lowered the binoculars.

They finished nine holes in two hours, then decided to buzz around in the cart to have a look at the North and South Courses. The layout of Waverly Creek was impressive, with fine homes tucked neatly against some of the fairways, a row of expensive condos wrapped around a small lake, a park for children, biking and jogging trails that crisscrossed the golf cart paths, and, most importantly, beautiful fairways and greens.

A foursome was teeing off at number fourteen when they approached. Golf etiquette demands silence around the tee, and Mr. Boone stopped the cart before he and Theo could be seen. When the golfers took off, Mr. Boone drove to the tee box. There was a watercooler, a trash can, and a ball cleaner at the edge of the cart path near a row of boxwoods.

Theo said, "According to Julio, his cousin saw the man drop the gloves into the trash can on number fourteen. This must be it."

"The cousin didn't tell you this?" Mr. Boone asked.

"No. I've talked to the cousin only once, Wednesday night at the shelter. Julio came to our office the following night with the gloves."

"So we have no idea where the cousin was or how or why he saw the man toss his gloves here at fourteen?"

"I guess not."

"And we're not sure why the cousin felt the need to get the gloves?"

"According to Julio, the boys who work out here always go through the trash."

They quickly took some photos, then eased away as another foursome approached.

CHAPTER 19

After golf, Theo and his father stopped by the Highland Street Shelter to check on Julio and his younger brother and sister. Carola Pena washed dishes in the kitchen of a downtown hotel and worked every Saturday, which meant her three children were left at the shelter. There were games and activities for the children who lived there, but Theo knew that Saturdays were not that pleasant. They watched a lot of television, played kick ball on the small playground, and, if lucky, rode a church bus to a cinema if a supervisor could find the money.

While Theo and his father were playing golf, they had an idea. Stratten College was a small private school that had been founded in the town a hundred years earlier. Its football and basketball teams couldn't compete with a decent high school, but its baseball team was a Division III powerhouse. There was a doubleheader at 2:00 p.m.

Mr. Boone checked in with the supervisor at the shelter. Not surprisingly, Julio, who was in charge of the twins, Hector and Rita, jumped at the chance to leave the shelter. The three practically ran to the SUV and jumped into the rear seat. Minutes later, Mr. Boone stopped at the hotel, parked illegally at the curb, and said, "I'll run and tell Mrs. Pena what we're doing." He was back in an instant, all smiles, and reported, "Your mother thinks it's a great idea."

"Thank you, Mr. Boone," Julio said. The twins were too excited to speak.

Stratten College played its games at Rotary Park, a wonderful old stadium on the edge of the town's center, near the small campus. Rotary Park was almost as old as the college and in years past had been the home to several minor league teams, none of which stayed very long. Its claim to fame was that a Hall of Famer, Ducky Medwick, had played one season there in 1920 with a Double A team before moving on to the Cardinals. There was a plaque near the front gate reminding fans of Ducky's brief stint in Strattenburg, but Theo had never seen anyone reading it.

Mr. Boone bought the tickets at a booth with only one window. The same old man had been working there since Ducky passed through. Three dollars for an adult, a dollar each for the kids. "How about some popcorn?" Mr. Boone asked as he looked down at the glowing faces of Hector and Rita. Five bags of popcorn, five sodas, twenty bucks. They walked up a ramp and into the bleachers, just down from the home dugout near first base. There were a lot of seats and few fans, and the ushers didn't care where they sat. The ballpark could hold two thousand, and the old-timers liked to brag about how big the crowds used to be. Theo watched five or six Stratten College games each season and had never seen the stadium even remotely close to half full. He loved the place, though, with its old-fashioned grandstand, overhanging roof, wooden bleachers close to the field, bull pens next to the foul lines, and an outfield wall covered with brightly painted ads for everything in Strattenburg from pest control to a local beer to lawyers in need of injured clients. A real ballpark.

There were those who wanted to tear it down. It was practically empty in the summertime, after the college season ended, and there were gripes about how much it cost for upkeep. This puzzled Theo because, looking around, it was hard to pinpoint exactly where any "upkeep" money was spent.

They stood for the national anthem, then Stratten College took the field. The four kids sat close together while Mr. Boone sat on the row behind them, listening. "All right," said Theo, the boss. "Nothing but English, okay? We're working on our English."

The Pena children naturally slid back into Spanish when chatting among themselves, but they instantly obeyed Theo and switched to English. Hector and Rita were eight years old and knew little about baseball. Theo began explaining.

Mrs. Boone and Ike arrived in the third inning and sat with Mr. Boone, who had eased away from the children. Theo tried to listen as they whispered among themselves. Ike had found an apartment, with rent of five hundred dollars a month. Mrs. Boone had not yet discussed the matter with Carola Pena because she was working at the hotel. They talked about other matters, but Theo couldn't catch it all.

Baseball can be boring for eight-year-olds who don't understand it, and by the fifth inning Hector and Rita were tossing popcorn and crawling around the bleachers. Mrs. Boone asked them if they wanted ice cream, and they jumped at the offer. When they left, Theo made his move. He asked Julio if he wanted to see the game from the center field bleachers. He said yes, and they drifted along the grandstand, past the bull pen, and eventually settled into an old section of seating just over the right center field wall. They were alone.

"I like the view from out here," Theo said. "Plus, it's always empty."

"I like it, too," Julio said.

They talked about the center fielder for a moment, then Theo changed subjects. "Look, Julio, we need to talk about your cousin. I can't remember his name. In fact, I'm not sure I've ever known his name."

"Bobby."

"Bobby?"

"It's really Roberto, but he likes to go by Bobby."

"Okay. Is his last name Pena?"

"No. His mother and my mother are sisters. His last name is Escobar."

"Bobby Escobar."

"*Sí.* Yes."

"Does he still work at the golf course?"

"Yes."

"And he still lives by the Quarry?"

"Yes. Why do you ask?"

"He's a very important person right now, Julio. He needs to come forward and tell the police everything he saw the day the woman was murdered."

Julio turned and looked at Theo as if he'd lost his mind. "He can't do that."

"Maybe he can. What if he could be promised protection? No arrest. No jail. Do you know what the word *immunity* means?"

"No."

"Well, in legal terms, it means he might be able to cut a deal with the police. If he comes forward and testifies, then the police won't bother him. He'll be immune. There may even be a way for him to get legal papers."

"Have you talked to the police?"

"No way, Julio."

"Have you told anyone?"

"I have protected his identity. He is safe, Julio. But I need to talk to him."

A player for the other team hit a ball that bounced off the right field wall. They watched him slide into third for a triple. Theo had to explain the difference between the ball going over the wall and one bouncing against it. Julio said there wasn't much baseball in El Salvador. Mainly soccer.

"When will you see Bobby again?" Theo asked.

"Tomorrow, maybe. He usually comes to the shelter on Sunday and we walk to church."

"Is there any way I can talk to him tonight?"

"I don't know. I don't know what he's doing all the time."

"Julio, time is crucial here."

"What's *crucial*?"

"Very important. The trial will be over on Monday. It's important for Bobby to come forward and tell what he saw."

"I don't think so."

"Julio, both of my parents are lawyers. You know them. They can be trusted. What if they were able to find an apartment for you and your family, including Bobby, a nice place just for you guys, and, at the same time, my parents take steps to sponsor Bobby so he can become legal? Think about it. No more hiding from the police. No more worrying about raids from the immigration people. You guys can all live together and Bobby will have papers. Wouldn't that be cool?"

Julio was staring into space, soaking it in. "That'd be awesome, Theo."

"Then here's what we do. First, you say it's okay to involve my parents. They'll be on your side. They're lawyers."

"Okay."

"Great. Next, you gotta see Bobby and convince him that this is a good deal. Convince him we can be trusted. Can you do that?"

"I don't know."

"Has he told your mother about what he saw?"

"Yes. She's like a mother to Bobby."

"Good. Get your mother to talk to him, too. She can convince him."

"You promise he won't go to jail?"

"I promise."

"But he has to talk to the police?"

"Maybe not the police, but he has to talk to someone involved with the trial. Maybe the judge. I don't know. But it's crucial for Bobby to come forward. He's the most important witness in this murder trial."

Julio placed his head in both hands, elbows on knees. His shoulders slumped under the weight of Theo's words and plans. For a long time nothing was said. Theo watched Hector and Rita in the distance, sitting with his mother and chatting away with their ice cream. Woods and Ike were deep in conversation, a rarity for them. The game dragged on.

"What do I do now?" Julio asked.

"Talk to your mother. Then both of you talk to Bobby. We should all get together."

"Okay."

CHAPTER
20

Theo was in the den watching a movie on cable when his cell phone vibrated in his pocket. It was eight thirty-five, Saturday night, and the call was coming from the shelter. He flipped the phone open, said, "Hello."

Julio's unmistakable voice said, "Theo?"

"Yes, Julio, what's up?" Theo muted the television. His father was in the study reading a novel and his mother was upstairs in bed, sipping green tea and reading through a pile of legal documents.

"I've talked to Bobby," Julio said, "and boy is he scared. The police were all over the Quarry today, checking papers, looking for trouble. They took in two boys from Guatemala, both illegal. Bobby thinks they're after him."

Theo walked to the study as he spoke. "Listen, Julio, if the police are after Bobby it has nothing to do with the murder trial. I can promise you that." Theo stood next to his father, who closed his book and listened closely.

"They went to his house, but he was hiding down the street."

"Did you talk to him, Julio? Did you tell him what we discussed today at the game?"

"Yes."

"And what did he say?"

"He's too scared right now, Theo. He doesn't understand how things work here. When he sees a policeman, he thinks bad things. You know? He thinks about going to jail, losing his job, his money, getting sent back home."

"Julio, listen to me," Theo said, frowning at his father. "He will not have to deal with the police. If he'll just trust me and my parents, he'll be safer. Did you explain this?"

"Yes."

"Does he understand it?"

"I don't know, Theo. But he wants to talk to you."

"Great. I'll talk to him." Theo nodded at his father and his father nodded back. "When and where?"

"Well, he's moving around tonight, not staying at his place. He's afraid the police might come back in the middle of the night and arrest them. But I can reach him."

Theo almost asked How? but let it go. "I think we should talk tonight," Theo said. His father nodded again.

"Okay. What do I tell him?"

"Tell him to meet me somewhere."

"Where?"

Theo couldn't think of a place fast enough. His father was a step ahead. He whispered, "Truman Park, by the carousel."

Theo said, "How about Truman Park?"

"Where's that?"

"It's the big park at the end of Main Street where they have the water fountains and statues and stuff like that. Anybody can find Truman Park."

"Okay."

"Tell him to be there at nine thirty, in about an hour. Meet us by the carousel."

"What's a carousel?"

"It's a fancy merry-go-round with little fake ponies and loud music. It's for small kids and their mothers."

"I've seen it."

"Good. Nine thirty."

The carousel was still spinning slowly late on Saturday night. Its well-used speakers boomed out the notes of "It's a

Small World" as a few toddlers and their mothers clutched the poles that ran down the center of the red and yellow ponies. Nearby there was a booth selling cotton candy and lemonade. A gang of young teenagers loitered about, all smoking and trying to look tough.

Woods Boone surveyed the area and felt it was safe. "I'll be waiting over there," he said, pointing to a tall bronze statue of a forgotten war hero. "You won't see me."

"I'll be fine," Theo said. He wasn't worried about safety. The park was well lit and well used.

Ten minutes later, Julio and Bobby Escobar eased from the shadows and saw Theo before he saw them. Bobby was very nervous and did not want to risk being seen by a policeman, so they walked to the other side of the park and found a spot on the steps of a gazebo. Theo couldn't see his father but he was sure he was watching.

He asked Bobby if he had worked that day, then went on to say that he and his father had played the Creek Course. No, Bobby had not worked, but instead had spent the day dodging cops. This opened the door, and Theo went charging through. He explained, in English, that Bobby had the opportunity to make a big change. He could move beyond being an illegal alien to a sponsored immigrant going through the process of getting proper documentation.

Julio rendered in Spanish. Theo understood little of it.

He explained that his parents were offering the deal of a lifetime. A better place to live, with family, the chance of a better job, and the fast track to being a legal resident. No more hiding from the police. No more fears about getting shipped home.

Julio rendered in Spanish. Bobby listened with a stone face, no expression at all.

Getting nothing in return, Theo pressed on. It was important to keep talking. Bobby seemed to be on the verge of running away. "Explain to him that he is a very important witness in the murder trial," Theo said to Julio. "And there is nothing wrong with going to court and telling everybody what he saw that day."

Julio rendered. Bobby nodded. He'd heard this before. He said something, which Julio translated as, "He doesn't want to get involved. This trial is not his problem."

A police car stopped at the edge of the park, not close to the gazebo but certainly close enough to be seen. Bobby watched it fearfully, as if he'd finally been caught. He mumbled quickly to Julio, who shot something back.

"The police are not after Bobby," Theo said. "Tell him to relax."

Two policemen crawled out of the car and began walking toward the center of the park, to the carousel. "See,"

Theo said. "The fat one is Ramsey Ross. All he does is write parking tickets. Don't know the other one. They couldn't care less about us."

Julio explained this in Spanish and Bobby began breathing again.

"Where will he stay tonight?" Theo asked.

"I don't know. He asked if he could sleep at the shelter, but there's no room."

"He can stay with us. We have an extra bedroom. You can come along, too. We'll call it a slumber party. My dad will stop and get us a pizza. Let's go."

At midnight, the three boys were sprawled around the den, yelling at the TV screen as they played a video game. Pillows and quilts were strewn about. Two large pizza boxes lay in ruins. Judge was munching on a crust.

From time to time, Marcella and Woods Boone peeked in. They were amused to hear Theo plow ahead with his Spanish, always a beat or two behind Julio and Bobby, but determined to catch up.

They had wanted more children, but nature didn't cooperate. And, at times, they had to admit that Theo was more than enough.

CHAPTER 21

Judge Gantry waited until it was dark early Sunday evening to go for a long walk. He lived a few blocks from the courthouse, in an old house that had been handed down from his grandfather, himself a distinguished judge, and he often roamed the streets in the center of Strattenburg in the early mornings and in the late evenings. On this night, he needed fresh air, time to think. The Duffy trial had consumed his weekend. He had spent hours buried in the law books looking for an answer, one that still eluded him. A heated argument raged within. Why should he disrupt a properly tried case? Why should he declare a mistrial when nothing had gone wrong? No rules had been broken. No ethics violated. Nothing. In fact, with two fine lawyers doing battle the trial had sailed smoothly along.

His research had revealed no similar case.

The lights were on at Boone & Boone. At seven thirty, as promised, Judge Gantry stepped onto the small front porch and knocked on the door.

It was opened by Marcella Boone, who said, "Well, good evening, Henry. Come in."

"Good evening, Marcella. I haven't seen this office in at least twenty years."

"Then you should stop by more often." She closed the door behind them.

Judge Gantry wasn't the only one having a brisk walk in the early evening. A man named Paco was out for a stroll, too. Paco wore a dark jogging suit, with running shoes, and he had a radio. He kept his distance and since the judge never thought about being followed, he was easy to trail. They roamed through central Strattenburg, one man deep in serious thought and oblivious to anyone around him, the other a block behind, carefully stalking as the shadows grew long and daylight disappeared. When Henry Gantry walked into Boone & Boone after dark, Paco jogged by the office, got the name and street number, and kept going until he turned the corner. Then he clicked a button on his two-way radio and said, "He's inside, at the Boones."

"Okay. I'm close by." The response came from Omar Cheepe.

Moments later, Cheepe picked up Paco, and they turned onto Park Street. When the Boone & Boone building was visible, they quietly eased into a parking place far down the street. Cheepe turned off the lights and the engine and rolled down his window for a smoke. "Did you see him go in?" he asked.

"No," Paco said. "I saw him turn off the sidewalk and head for the front door. I know he's in there. It's the only place open along here."

"Very strange."

It was Sunday night, and the other office buildings were dark and deserted. Only the Boone firm showed signs of activity. All of its downstairs lights appeared to be on.

"What do you think they're doing?" Paco asked.

"Not sure. The Boones were in Gantry's office Friday, the whole family, which makes no sense because Gantry was very busy. They're not criminal lawyers, you know. He drafts deeds and she handles divorces, so there's no reason to barge into Gantry's office in the middle of a murder trial.

And the kid, I just don't get it. Why would the parents take the kid out of school and in to see Gantry? The kid's been hanging around all week, snooping around the trial."

"This is Theo?"

"Yep. Kid thinks he's a lawyer. Knows every cop, every judge, every court clerk. Hangs around courtrooms, probably knows more law than most lawyers. He and Gantry are big pals. He goes to see Gantry, with his parents, and, suddenly, Gantry decides not to hold court on Saturday, after promising all week. Something's going on here, Paco. And it's not in our favor."

"You talked to Nance or Mr. Duffy?"

"No, not yet. Here's what we do. I would almost send you up there to poke around the building, look inside, see who's there, but it's too risky. They see you, they get spooked, they stop whatever they're doing, maybe they call the cops. It is Judge Gantry, you know. Things could get complicated. So here's a better plan. I'll call Gus and get the van. We can park it closer up the street, and when they come out we take pictures. I want to know who's in there."

"Who do you think?"

"Don't know, Paco, but I'll bet a hundred bucks the Boone family and Gantry are not in there playing gin rummy. Something's going on here, and I don't like it."

———

Judge Gantry walked to the library, where Mr. Boone, Ike, and Theo were waiting. The long table that dominated the room was covered with books, maps, notepads, and gave the impression that a lot of work was under way. Everyone shook hands, said their hellos. There was some small talk about the weather, but with important matters looming the chitchat didn't last long.

"Needless to say," Judge Gantry said after they were all seated, "this little meeting is off the record. We're doing nothing wrong, mind you, since you're not involved in the case. But, I can hear a lot of questions being asked if word got out. Understood?"

"Of course, Henry," Mrs. Boone said.

"No problem," Ike said.

"Not a word," Mr. Boone said.

"Yes, sir," Theo said.

"Good. Now, you said that you have something to show me."

The three adult Boones looked at Theo, who immediately jumped to his feet. His laptop was on the table in front of him. He touched a key, and a large photo appeared on the digital wide-screen whiteboard at the end of the room. Theo held a laser pointer and directed the red light at the photo. "This is an aerial photo of the sixth fairway at the Creek Course. Over here is the Duffy home. Over here, in the trees in the dogleg, is where the witness was sitting and having lunch." He pressed another key, another photo appeared. "This is a photo we took yesterday morning at the golf course. The witness was sitting on this stack of treated timbers, next to the dry streambed, completely hidden from view. However"—another key, another photo—"as you can see, the witness had a perfect view of the homes on the other side of the fairway, about a hundred yards away."

"And you know for certain this is exactly where he was?"

"Yes, sir."

"Can you reconstruct the time?"

"Yes, Your Honor."

"We can drop the 'Your Honor' stuff, Theo, for the time being."

"Okay." Another photo, an aerial. Theo beamed the laser light at a building. "This is the maintenance shed, not too far through the woods from the sixth fairway. The lunch break began at eleven thirty. Eleven thirty on the dot because the supervisor ran a tight ship and expected his workers to check in at eleven thirty, eat quickly, and be back on the job at noon. Our man liked to sneak away from the others, eat by himself, say his prayers, and look at a photo of his family back home. He's very homesick. As you can see, it's a short walk through the woods to his favorite lunch spot. He estimates that he was halfway through his lunch break when he saw the man enter the Duffy home."

"So around eleven forty-five?" Judge Gantry asked.

"Yes, sir. And, as you know, the pathologist put the time of death at approximately eleven forty-five."

"I know. And the man who entered the house then left it before your witness finished his lunch break?"

"Yes, sir. The witness says that he usually heads back to the maintenance shed a few minutes before noon. On this day, he saw the man come out of the house before he finished the lunch break. He estimates the man was in the house less than ten minutes."

"I have one big question," the judge said. "Did this witness see the man leave the house with a bag or sack or anything that might hold the stolen loot? The testimony is that several items were taken—two small handguns, some of her jewelry, and at least three of his expensive watches. Did the witness see this stuff hauled away?"

"I don't think so, Judge," Theo said gravely. "And, I've thought about this for hours. My best guess is that he stuffed the guns under his belt, hid them with his sweater, and put everything else in his pockets."

"What kind of guns?" Mr. Boone asked.

"A nine millimeter and a snub-nosed thirty-eight," Judge Gantry said. "It would be easy to hide them under a sweater."

"And the watches and jewelry?"

"Some rings and necklaces, three watches with leather bands. All could fit easily into the front pockets of a pair of slacks."

"And this stuff was never found?" Mrs. Boone asked.

"No."

"They're probably at the bottom of one of those lakes out there at the golf course," Ike said with a nasty grin.

"You're probably right," Judge Gantry said, to the amazement of everyone else. The stone-faced referee who never leaned to one side or the other had just tipped his hand. He thought Mr. Pete Duffy was guilty after all.

"What about the gloves?" he asked.

Theo picked up a small brown box, sat it on the table, and then pulled out the Ziploc plastic bag holding the two golf gloves. He placed it in front of Judge Gantry, and for a second or two everyone stared at the evidence as if it were a bloody butcher's knife. Theo pressed a key, and another photo appeared on the screen. "This is the fourteenth tee box, South Nine. The witness was repairing a sprinkler head right about here, on a small hill overlooking the tee box, when he saw the man, the same man, remove these two gloves from his golf bag and throw them in the trash basket."

"A question," Judge Gantry said. "At the moment he tossed away these gloves, was he wearing another set of gloves?" It was obvious to the Boones that the judge had dissected every detail of the story.

"I've never asked him that question," Theo said.

"Probably so," Woods said. "It's not unusual for a golfer to keep extra gloves in his bag."

"Why would that matter?" Mrs. Boone asked.

"Not sure that it would. I'm just very curious right now, Marcella."

There was a long pause, as if those present were thinking the same thing but no one wanted to mention it. Finally, Theo said, "Judge, you could always ask the witness."

"So he's here?"

"Yes, sir."

"He's in my office, Henry," Mrs. Boone said. "He's now represented by the Boone law firm."

"Does that include Theo?" Judge Gantry asked, and everyone thought it was somewhat funny.

"You have to assure us, Henry, that he will not be arrested or prosecuted for anything," Mr. Boone said.

"You have my word," Judge Gantry said.

Bobby Escobar sat across the table from the judge. To his left was Julio, his cousin and interpreter, and to his right was his aunt Carola. It was a family affair with Hector and Rita back in Mrs. Boone's office watching television.

Theo began his direct examination with the same aerial photo of the sixth fairway, Creek Course. With the red laser light, he and Bobby pinpointed the exact spot where he'd been eating his lunch. Theo changed photos, asked his questions carefully, and gave Julio plenty of time to translate. The story unfolded perfectly.

Woods, Marcella, and Ike sat back and watched with enormous pride, but all three were ready to catch any mistake.

Once the facts were established and Bobby had established himself as a reliable witness, Judge Gantry said, "Now, let's talk about identification."

Since Bobby had never met Pete Duffy, he could not say that he was the man who entered the house. He did say that the man was wearing a black sweater, tan slacks, and a maroon golf cap, the same outfit Pete Duffy was wearing at the time of the murder. Theo flashed up a series of photos of Pete Duffy, all taken from the newspaper. To each, Bobby could only say that the man in the photo definitely resembled the man he'd seen. Theo pressed another key and ran three quick videos he'd strung together, all showing Pete Duffy either walking into the courthouse or walking out. Again, Bobby said he was almost certain that was the man.

Then, the clincher. The prosecution had placed into evidence twenty-two photographs of the crime scene, the house, and the neighborhood. One of the photos, State's Exhibit No. 15, had been taken from a position somewhere near the edge of the fairway. It showed the rear of the Duffy home, its patio, windows, rear door, and off to the far right there were two uniformed policeman standing next to a golf cart. Sitting in the golf cart was Pete Duffy, who appeared dazed and distraught. The photo had apparently been taken just minutes after he raced home from the Clubhouse Grill.

Theo had obtained the photograph by "visiting" the site maintained by the court reporting service. If Judge Gantry asked how he got it, Theo was prepared to say, "Well, Judge, it's been produced in open court and admitted into evidence. Not really a secret, is it?"

But Judge Gantry said nothing. He'd seen the photo a hundred times and was unmoved by it. Bobby, though, had never seen it, and he immediately began speaking rapidly to Julio.

"That's him," Julio said, actually pointing. "The man in the cart. That's him."

"Let the record show, Your Honor, that the witness has just identified the defendant, Mr. Peter Duffy."

"Got it, Theo," Gantry said.

CHAPTER 22

The spectators gathered Monday morning for the final drama. The jurors arrived with solemn faces, determined to finish the job. The lawyers wore their finest suits and appeared fresh and eager to get their verdict. The defendant himself looked rested, confident. The clerks and bailiffs hustled about with their usual early morning energy. But when they grew still, at ten minutes after 9:00 a.m., the courtroom seemed to inhale and wait. Everyone stood when Judge Gantry entered, his black robe flowing behind. He said, "Please be seated," and did not smile. He was not happy. He seemed very tired.

He looked around the courtroom, nodded at his court

reporter, acknowledged his jury, noticed the crowd and in particular looked at the third row, right side. There was Theo Boone, wedged between his father and his uncle, absent from school, at least for the moment. Judge Gantry looked at Theo and their eyes locked. Then he leaned down a few inches closer to the microphone. He cleared his throat and began to deliver the words no one expected.

"Good morning, ladies and gentlemen. At this point in the trial of Mr. Peter Duffy, we are scheduled to hear the closing arguments from the lawyers. However, this will not happen. For reasons that I will not explain at this moment, I am declaring a mistrial."

There were gasps, jolts, shocked expressions from all corners of the courtroom. Theo was watching Pete Duffy, whose jaw dropped to his chest as he turned to Clifford Nance. The lawyers on both sides appeared to have been hit between the eyes, all staggering as they tried to understand what they had just heard. On the front row, directly behind the defense table, Omar Cheepe turned and looked straight at Theo, two rows back. He didn't stare, didn't look particularly menacing, but his timing said it all—"You did this. I know it. And I'm not finished."

The jurors were not sure what would happen next, so Judge Gantry explained it to them. He turned, looked at them, and said, "Members of the jury, a mistrial means that the trial is over. The charges against Mr. Peter Duffy are dismissed, but only for the moment. The charges will be filed again, and there will be another trial in the very near future, but with a different jury. In any criminal trial, the judge has the absolute discretion to declare a mistrial when he or she believes that something has happened that might adversely affect the final verdict. Such is the case now. I thank you for your service. You are important to our judicial system. You are now excused."

The jurors were thoroughly bewildered, but some were beginning to understand that their civic duty was over. A bailiff herded them through a side door. As they shuffled out, Theo watched and admired Judge Gantry. At that moment, he, Theo, decided that he wanted to be a great judge, just like his hero up there on the bench. A judge who knew the law inside and out and believed in fairness, but, more importantly, a judge who could make the tough decision.

"Told you so," Ike whispered. Ike had been convinced that a mistrial would be declared, but then so had the rest of the Boone law firm.

The jurors left but no one else moved. They were stunned and wanted more information. At the same time, Jack Hogan and Clifford Nance rose slowly and looked at Judge Gantry.

Before either could speak, he said, "Gentlemen, I will not explain my actions at this time. Tomorrow, at ten a.m., we will meet in my office and I will state my reasons. I want the charges refiled as soon as possible. I will schedule the retrial for the third week in June. The defendant will remain free on bond with the same restrictions. Court is adjourned." He slapped his gavel on the bench, stood, and then vanished.

With the judge and jury gone, there wasn't much left to do. The crowd slowly climbed to its feet and headed for the door.

"Get to school," Mr. Boone said sternly to Theo.

Outside the courthouse, Theo unchained his bike. "You stopping by this afternoon?" Ike asked.

"Sure," Theo said. "It's Monday."

"We need to debrief. It's been a long week."

"Sure has."

Not far away, at the front entrance, there was noise and the rush of people trying to get out of the courthouse. Pete Duffy, surrounded by his lawyers and others, hustled away with a couple of reporters yelling questions at him. The questions were not answered. Omar Cheepe brought up the rear, and actually shoved one of the reporters. He was about to take off with his client when he noticed Theo, straddling his bike, watching the drama with Ike. Cheepe froze, and for a split second seemed undecided about what to do. Should he hurry and protect Mr. Duffy, or should he walk over to Theo and utter a vile threat or two?

Theo and Cheepe stared at each other, fifty feet apart, then Cheepe turned and scampered away. Ike seemed not to notice this exchange.

Theo hurried away, too. He headed for school, and once the courthouse was far behind him, he began to relax. He found it difficult to believe that it was Monday. So much had happened in the past seven days. The biggest trial in the town's history had come and gone, yet it wasn't over. Thanks to Theo, a bad verdict had been avoided. Justice had been preserved, at least for the time being. He would take a break from his duties, but before long he would be meeting secretly with Bobby Escobar and Julio. No doubt about it. Theo would be in charge of coaching Bobby, preparing him for the three hours he would spend on the witness stand come June.

And now Omar the Creep was complicating things. How much did he and his client and Clifford Nance really know? Questions, questions. Theo was puzzled, but he was already excited.

Then he thought of April. Tomorrow, Tuesday, the judge would issue a ruling that would require her to live with one parent or the other. Her presence would not be required in court, but she was a wreck anyway. Theo needed to spend some time with her. He decided that they would sneak away at lunch and talk about things.

And he thought about Woody, whose brother was in jail and likely to stay there.

He parked his bike at the flagpole and walked into the school halfway through first period. He had a written excuse from his mother, and as he handed it over to Miss Gloria in the front office he noticed that she wasn't smiling. She always smiled.

"Have a seat, Theo," she said, nodding to a wooden chair beside her desk.

But why? Theo wondered. It's just a simple matter of being tardy.

"How was the funeral?" she asked, still unsmiling.

A pause, as Theo tried to understand. "I'm sorry."

"The funeral last Friday, the one your uncle came here . . ."

"Oh, that funeral. It was great. A real blast."

She looked around nervously, then tapped her lips with an index finger. *Please talk softly,* she was saying. There were open office doors nearby.

"Theo," she almost whispered. "My brother was stopped last night for driving under the influence. They took him to jail." She rolled her eyes around to make sure they were alone.

"I'm sorry," Theo said. He knew where this was going.

"He's not a drunk. He's a grown man with a wife and kids and a good job. He's never been in trouble and we just don't know what to do."

"What was his BAC?"

"What?"

"His blood alcohol content."

"Oh, that. Does point zero nine sound right?"

"Yes. The limit is point zero eight, so he's in trouble. First offense?"

"Why heavens yes, Theo. He's not a drunk. He barely had two glasses of wine."

Two drinks. Always two drinks. Regardless of how drunk or how sloppy or how belligerent, they've never had more than two drinks.

"The policeman said he could get ten days in jail," she went on. "This is so embarrassing."

"Which cop?" Theo asked.

"How am I supposed to know that?"

"Some of the cops like to scare people. Your brother will not get ten days. He'll pay a fine of six hundred dollars, lose his license for six months, go to driving school, and a year from now his record can be expunged. Did he spend the entire night in jail?"

"Yes. I can't imagine . . ."

"Then there's no more jail time. Write down this name." She was already holding a pen. "Taylor Baskin," Theo said. "He's the lawyer who handles all the drunks . . ."

"He's not a drunk!" she said, a bit too loud. Both looked around to see if anyone was listening. No one.

"Sorry. Taylor Baskin is the drunk driving lawyer. Your brother needs to call him."

Miss Gloria was scribbling away.

"I need to get to class," Theo said.

"Thank you, Theo. Please don't tell anyone."

"No problem. Can I go now?"

"Oh, yes, please. And thanks, Theo."

He scampered out of the office, leaving behind another satisfied client.

For more exciting legal drama,
catch **THEODORE BOONE**'s
next adventure . . .

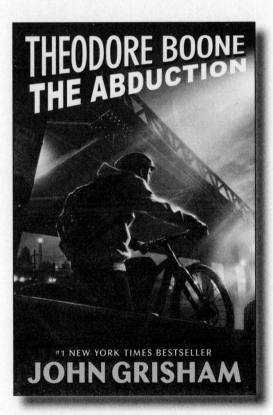

CHAPTER 1

The abduction of April Finnemore took place in the dead of night, sometime between 9:15 p.m., when she last spoke with Theo Boone, and 3:30 a.m., when her mother entered her bedroom and realized she was gone. The abduction appeared to have been rushed; whoever took April did not allow her to gather her things. Her laptop was left behind. Though her bedroom was fairly neat, there was some clothing strewn about, which made it difficult to determine if she had been able to pack. Probably not, the police thought. Her toothbrush was still by the sink. Her backpack was by her bed. Her pajamas were on the floor, so she at least had been allowed to change. Her mother, when she wasn't crying or ranting, told the police that her daughter's favorite blue-and-white sweater was not in the closet. And April's favorite sneakers were gone, too.

The police soon dismissed the notion that she'd simply run away. There was no reason to run away, her mother assured them, and she had not packed the things that would make such an escape successful.

A quick inspection of the home revealed no apparent break-in. The windows were all closed and locked, as were the three doors downstairs. Whoever took April was careful enough to close the door behind them, and lock it on the way out. After observing the scene and listening to Mrs. Finnemore for about an hour, the police decided to have a talk with Theo Boone. He was, after all, April's best friend, and they usually chatted by phone or online at night before going to sleep.

At the Boone home, the phone rang at 4:33, according to the digital clock next to the bed where the parents slept. Mr. Woods Boone, the lighter sleeper, grabbed the phone, while Mrs. Marcella Boone rolled over and began wondering who would call at such an hour. When Mr. Boone said, "Yes, Officer," Mrs. Boone really woke up and scrambled out of bed. She listened to his end of the conversation, soon understood that it had something to do with April Finnemore, and was really confused when her husband said, "Sure, Officer, we can be over there in fifteen minutes." He hung up, and she said, "What is it, Woods?"

"Apparently, April's been abducted, and the police would like to talk to Theo."

Even a future star lawyer
like **THEODORE BOONE**
has to deal with statewide
standardized testing—

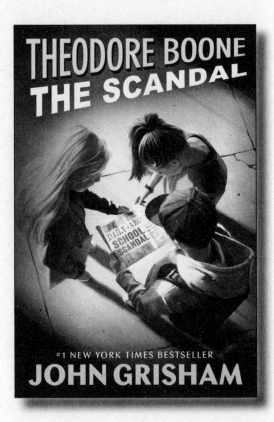

CHAPTER 1

Theodore Boone woke up in a foul mood. In fact, he'd gone to bed in a foul mood, and things had not improved during the night. As a few rays of morning sun lit his room, he stared at the ceiling and tried to think of ways to avoid this entire week. Generally, he enjoyed school—his friends, the teachers, most of the classes, debating—but there were times when he just wanted to stay in bed. This was one of those times, the worst week of the year. Beginning tomorrow, Tuesday, and running through Friday, he and every other eighth grader would be stuck at their desks taking a series of dreadful tests.

Judge knew something was wrong, and at some point had left his spot beside Theo's bed and assumed his spot on top of the covers. Mrs. Boone frowned on the idea of the dog sleeping in Theo's bed, but she was downstairs having her quiet time with the morning newspaper and wouldn't know. Or would she? Occasionally she noticed dog hair on the covers and asked Theo if Judge was sleeping with him. Most of the time Theo said yes, but quickly followed the admission with the question: "What am I supposed to do?" He couldn't watch the dog while he, Theo, was sound asleep. And, to be honest, Theo didn't really want the dog in the bed with him. Judge had the irritating habit of stretching himself out smack in the middle of things and expecting Theo to retreat to the edges, where he often came within inches of crashing to the floor and waking up with a sore head. No, Theo preferred that Judge sleep on his little doggy bed down below.

The truth was, Judge did whatever he wanted to do, and not only in Theo's room but in every room in the house.

On days like today, Theo envied his dog. What a life: no school, no homework, no tests, no pressure. He ate whenever he wanted, napped most of the day at the office, and seemed unconcerned about most things. The Boones took care of his needs, and he did anything he wanted.

Reluctantly, Theo got out of bed, rubbed his dog's head, said good morning, but not with as much enthusiasm as usual, and went to the bathroom. Last week the orthodontist had readjusted his braces, and his jaws still ached. He grinned at himself in the mirror, took stock of the mouthful of metal that he despised, and tried to find hope in the fact that he *might* get the braces off just in time to start the ninth grade.

He stepped into the shower and thought about the ninth grade. High school. He just wasn't ready for it. He was thirteen and quite content at Strattenburg Middle School, where he liked his teachers, most of them anyway, and was captain of the Debate Team, almost an Eagle Scout and, well, thought of himself as a leader. He was certainly the only kid lawyer in the school, the only kid he knew of who dreamed of being either a big-time trial lawyer or a brilliant young judge. He couldn't make up his mind. In the ninth grade he would be just another lowly freshman at the bottom of the pile. Freshmen got no respect in high school. Middle school was okay because Theo had found his place, a place that would disappear in a few months. High school was all about football, basketball, cheerleaders, driving, dating, band, theatre, large classes, clothes, shaving, and, well, growing up. He just wasn't ready for it. Most of his friends wanted to hurry along and grow up, but not Theo.

He stepped out of the shower and dried off. Judge was watching him and thinking about nothing but breakfast. Such a lucky dog.

As Theo brushed his teeth, or rather cleaned his braces, he admitted that life was changing. High school was slowly rising on the horizon. One of its most important and unpleasant warning signs was standardized testing, a horrible idea cooked up by some experts far away. Those people had decided that it was important to give the same tests at the same time to every eighth grader in the state so that the folks in charge of Strattenburg Middle School and all the other schools would know how they stacked up. That was one reason for the tests. Another reason, at least in Strattenburg, was to separate the eighth graders into three groups for high school. The smartest would be fast-tracked into an Honors program. The weaker students would be placed on a slower track. And the average kids would be treated normally and allowed to enjoy high school without special treatment.

Yet another reason for the tests was to measure how well the teachers were doing. If a teacher's class did really well, he or she would qualify for a bonus. And if the class did poorly, all kinds of bad things might happen to the teacher. He or she might even be fired.

Needless to say, the entire process of testing, scoring, tracking, and evaluating teachers had become hotly controversial. The students, of course, hated it. Most of the teachers didn't like it. Almost all parents wanted their kids in the Honors classes, and almost all were disappointed. Those with kids on the "slow track" were mad, even embarrassed.

And so the debate raged. Mrs. Boone was firmly opposed to the testing, so, of course, Mr. Boone supported it. The family had talked about testing for weeks, over dinner and in the car, and even while watching television. For a month, the eighth-grade teachers had been preparing the students for the tests. "Teaching to the tests," was the favorite description, which meant no creative teaching was being done and no one was having fun in class.

Theo was already sick of the tests, and they had not even started.

He dressed, grabbed his backpack, and went downstairs, Judge at his heels. He said hello to his mother, who, as always, was curled up on the sofa in her robe, sipping coffee and reading the newspaper. Mr. Boone always left early and joined his friends for coffee and gossip at the same downtown diner.

Theo fixed two bowls of Cheerios and put one on the floor for Judge. They almost always ate in silence, but occasionally Mrs. Boone joined them for a chat. She did this when she suspected something was bothering Theo. Today, she entered the kitchen, poured more coffee, and took a seat across from her son. "What's up today?" she asked.

"More reviewing, more practicing how to take the tests."

"Are you nervous?"

"Not really. I'm just tired already. I don't do well on these tests, so I don't like them."

It was true. Theo was almost a straight-A student, with an occasional B in the sciences, but he had never done well on standardized tests. "What if I don't make the Honors track next year?" he asked.

"Teddy, you're going to excel in high school, college, and law school, if you choose to go there. Don't worry about where they put you in the ninth grade."

"Thanks, Mom." Her words felt good in spite of the fact that she called him "Teddy," a little nickname that, thankfully, only she used, and only when they were alone.

Theo had friends whose parents were turning flips and losing sleep over the tests. If their kids didn't make Honors, the parents were convinced their kids were headed for miserable lives. The whole thing seemed silly to Theo.

She said, "I suppose you know that there is a backlash across the country against these tests. They are becoming very unpopular, and there appears to be widespread cheating."

"How do you cheat on a standardized test?"

"I'm not sure, but I've read about some of the cheating. In one district the teachers changed answers. Hard to believe, isn't it?"

"Why would a teacher do that?"

"Well, in that case, the school was not very good and on probation with the district. Plus, the teachers wanted to qualify for a bonus. None of it makes any sense."

"I think I'm getting sick. Do I look pale?"

"No, Teddy. You look perfectly healthy."

It was eight o'clock, time to move. Theo rinsed both bowls and left them in the sink, same as always. He kissed his mom on the cheek and said, "I'm off."

"Do you have lunch money?" she asked, the same question five days a week.

"Always."

"And your homework is complete?"

"It's perfect, Mom."

"And I'll see you when?"

"I'll stop by the office after school." Theo stopped by the office every day after school, without fail, but Mrs. Boone always asked.

"Be careful," she said. "And remember to smile."

"I'm smiling, Mom."

"Love you, Teddy."

"Love you back."

Theo stepped outside and said good-bye to Judge, who would ride in the car with Mrs. Boone to the office where he would spend his day sleeping and eating and worrying about nothing. Theo jumped on his bike and sped away, once again wishing he could be a dog for the next four days.

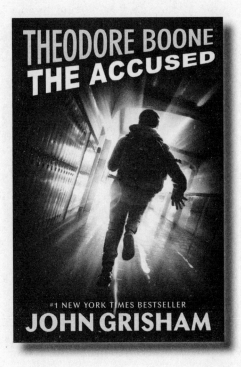

THEODORE BOONE
THE ACCUSED

#1 NEW YORK TIMES BESTSELLER
JOHN GRISHAM

Theo Boone might only be thirteen, but he's already uncovered key evidence in a groundbreaking murder trial and discovered the truth behind his best friend's abduction. Now with the latest unfolding of events in Strattenburg, Theo will face his biggest challenge yet.

As all of Strattenburg sits divided over a hot political and environmental issue, Theo finds himself in the middle of the battle. The county commission is fighting hard to change the landscape of the town, and Theo is strongly against the plans. When he uncovers corruption beneath the surface, Theo will confront bigger risks than ever to himself and those he loves. But even face-to-face with danger, Theodore Boone will do whatever it takes to stand up for what is right.

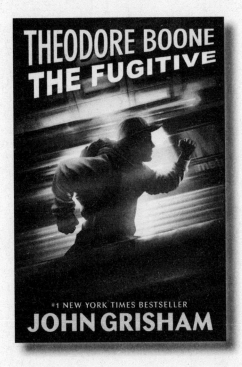

On a field trip to Washington, DC, Theo spots a familiar face on the Metro: accused murderer and fugitive Pete Duffy, who jumped bail and was never seen again. Theo's quick thinking helps bring Duffy back to Strattenburg to stand trial. But now that Duffy knows who he is, Theo is in greater danger than he's ever been in before. Even when everything is on the line, Theodore Boone will stop at nothing to make sure a killer is brought to justice.